KIDNAPPED

"There's but one thing I want," Captain Lawrence said. "One thing only. Then you can sail away." Lawrence took a step toward Rosie.

Sauntering toward her, he took her chin in his hand. She wrenched it away and he recaptured it cruelly. "You can send your Captain Lyons after me." He laughed. "I'd be delighted to show him my prize."

The sailors around Rosie tightened their circle. "Gentlemen," Lawrence said, stopping before Rosie and her protectors. "I advise you to step aside. If you make any moves which might be misunderstood, my mate will have no choice but to blow off your captain's head."

Rosie lifted her chin high, but inside she was trembling. "I'll go with you," she said. "Don't hurt anybody."

Other Avon Flare Books in the
AMERICAN DREAMS *Series*

PLAINSONG FOR CAITLIN *by Elizabeth M. Rees*
SARAH ON HER OWN *by Karen M. Coombs*

Coming Soon

SONG OF THE SEA *by Jean Ferris*

AMERICAN DREAMS

Into the Wind

JEAN FERRIS

AN AVON FLARE BOOK

INTO THE WIND is an original publication of Avon Books. This work has never before appeared in book form.

AVON BOOKS
A division of
The Hearst Corporation
1350 Avenue of the Americas
New York, New York 10019

First Avon Flare Printing: May 1996

AVON FLARE TRADEMARK REG. U.S. PAT. OFF. AND IN OTHER COUNTRIES, MARCA REGISTRADA, HECHO EN U.S.A.

Printed in the U.S.A.

RA 10 9 8 7 6 5 4 3 2 1

For A.G.F.

Author's Note

Dear Reader:

It's easy to forget that history, which sounds like such an important and intimidating thing, is actually only events being lived by people like you and me and our friends and relatives. Someday, whatever you're doing right now will be considered history—no matter how hip and with it your current haircut, wardrobe or lifestyle, it will be history, quaint and gone.

It's the lives of ordinary people, living through the events of their time, that interest me. They faced many of the same problems we do today: getting along with others, making a living, deciding which side to be on in a conflict, acting with courage or cowardice in the face of trouble. Sometimes they got it right and sometimes they didn't. And then, as now, there were bad people and weak people and misguided people who messed things up for those trying to do the right thing. And these ordinary people are usually ignored by history books, passed over in favor of more famous names.

The rush and highly developed technology of today's world make it hard to find room for things that take time and close personal contact: romance, long conversations, letter writing, storytelling, games. We must not forget how to do these things, and reading novels about people doing them is one way to remember. These people of the past can teach us, too, by their example— revealed in their diaries and letters—of how they faced the same problems of life that we encounter today.

Rosie, Raider and the other characters in the *Into the Wind* books are real people to me, looking for love and self-respect, and some good times, too—just like us. I hope they will be as real to you.

Jean Ferris

Chapter 1

Campeche, the Yucatán, Mexico
April 17, 1814

It was barely light when Rosie left the Drop Anchor with the basket of dresses heavy on her arm, but already the harbor was busy with shrimpers setting out for a day's work and logwood being loaded noisily into the holds of ships. Anchored farther out in the quiet bay were several English and American warships uneasily sharing the waters of the neutral port. But Rosie sometimes found it hard to believe the port was supposed to be neutral; she saw fights between English and American seaman almost every night at the Drop Anchor, the cantina her father operated outside the walls of Campeche.

The cantina he pretended to operate, was more the truth. In reality, *she* was the one who did most of the work. Rosie's bare heels kicked up little puffs of dust along the path to La Señora's; little, *furious* puffs of dust, she imagined them to be, to match her state of mind.

Her eyes were scratchy with sleeplessness and her head still rang with the latest argument with her father.

1

The argument about the same thing they'd argued over so many times before—his refusal to abide by the established closing hour so that she could do some cleaning up before going to bed. Instead, he wanted to sit at one of the scarred tables with the customers, drinking *x-tabentum,* the potent Mayan drink made from fermented honey, knowing he wouldn't be the one to rise early in order to get the day's chores done. It incensed her, the way he acted so oppressed and put upon when she wanted to close up, as if she were the demanding parent and he the innocent child.

She mumbled words in Spanish under her breath, words she wasn't supposed to know, and kicked her heels harder, making even bigger puffs of dust. Because she was watching her feet, she didn't see the elaborate wrought-iron gate open in the high wall around La Señora's flower-filled courtyard and pink-washed house. Nor did she see the tall figure who came striding rapidly through the gate, so rapidly he was unable to avoid colliding directly into her.

She sat down hard on the dusty path, her basket dropping, upsetting the dresses and all her sewing supplies. She looked up at him and released her emotions in a string of colorful Spanish curses.

He listened to her for a while before he said in Spanish, but with a heavy American accent, "That's quite a vocabulary for a little girl."

She showed him a bit more of her vocabulary before adding in English, "And I'm not a little girl. I'm seventeen. And the least you can do is help me pick these things up." On her knees, her favorite skirt now streaked with dirt, she retrieved one of the spilled dresses. "Oh, look what you've done. It's filthy!"

He took it from her and shook it so hard the fabric gave off the crack of a pistol. He held it at arm's length. "Looks fine to me."

2

She scrambled to her feet and snatched the dress from him. Holding it out, she could see that he had, indeed, shaken all the dust from it.

"Well, do the same with the rest of them," she ordered.

One of his dark eyebrows went up, along with the corner of his mouth, but he merely said, "Yes, ma'am," and went to work.

She refolded the dresses one by one and returned them to her basket. What could you expect from the kind of man who patronized La Señora's, anyway? She knew what the girls there did with the sailors from the ships. She knew why the pious Campechan mamas kept their daughters from going near the pink house. Well, she had a living to earn, and no mama to protect her, so she had to come here. But she wouldn't allow this tall young man with the seaman's tan to think she was like the girls who lived at La Señora's. She only sold the products of her needle to them.

"My supplies, too," she directed him, pointing to the spilled sewing articles on the path.

"Yes, ma'am," he said again, and squatted easily, balancing on his booted toes as he collected pincushions and scissors, a needle case and a measuring tape, lengths of lace and spools of thread.

"I'm a seamstress," she said.

"Really. I never would have guessed." His eyebrow quirked up again as a beam of sunlight came over the top of La Señora's house, brightening his brown hair to dark gold. His light brown eyes were sparked with gold, too, giving them a glint of humor and intelligence, which for some reason made her furious all over again.

"Do you have a name?" he asked.

She raised her chin. "It's Rosalia Maria-Luisa Unity Fielding." Her name alone, she felt, distinguished her from La Señora's girls, who were called such things as

3

Pinky and Lalo and Anna-Bird. And then she felt an immediate flash of guilt as she thought of how good La Señora and her girls had always been to her, how promptly they paid their bills, how sometimes they gossiped with her or arranged her hair. They were certainly better than the pious Campechan mamas who hadn't let their children play with the daughter of a cantina owner, and who now looked sideways at her because she worked in the cantina. They'd be surprised to know the way their sons looked at her, she thought sourly.

"That name's bigger than you are," he said. "I'm afraid I have nothing so grand to offer. I'm plain Robert Lyons."

"Well, good-bye, *Señor* Lyons," she said, hefting her basket onto her arm and turning into the gate he had just come through.

He gave her a salute and stood in the dust, the sunlight gilding him as she swung the gate closed. "Good-bye, Nettle," he said.

Nettle, she thought, crossing the swept earth of the courtyard. Well, all right. She knew she was difficult and prickly. But that was only because she wanted so badly to get out of Campeche. She hated Campeche, in spite of its beautiful beaches and wonderful assortment of shells. She'd wanted to get out since she arrived at five with her footloose, restless father.

Well, that wasn't exactly so. At first, she'd been glad to stop for a while after the two years of constant traveling following the death of her Portuguese mother. But the Mexican children made fun of her because she couldn't speak Spanish, and when she could, they weren't allowed to play with her because she lived above the Drop Anchor. Father Xavier and Chila, his housekeeper, had been her friends for a while, but Fa-

4

ther Xavier had gone to the Cathedral in Mérida seven years before, just after Chila had died from the fever.

She sighed and pushed open the heavy wooden door to La Señora's casa. The cool, quiet air from within breathed over her, soothing her. She stood on the threshold, dimness and silence before her, the hot Mexican morning on her back, the heavy fragrance of the mammoth roses in La Señora's patio surrounding her. Beyond the pink house, beyond the walls of Campeche, the jungles of the Yucatán waited, hiding Mayan ruins and prowling ocelots.

"Rosie? Is that you?" La Señora called. "You're so early." She came across the tiled floor like a ship in full sail, her opulent body overflowing her gown. She took Rosie's free hand in both her own and pulled her into the big front parlor, where she pressed her down onto a richly upholstered Jacobean sofa, the gift of a grateful seafarer she always referred to as The Corsair. "I was just about to have my morning chocolate. You'll have some, too." She sailed away to fetch the chocolate.

Rosie sat in the hushed room, waiting. She couldn't help it, she loved the way La Señora fussed over her, the way she imagined her own mother would have if she'd lived. There seemed to be a permanent bruise on her heart from losing her mother before she had been able to fix a single memory of her in her mind. All she had now was a miniature painting in a locket, and an imagination that conjured bittersweet shadows and fantasy.

La Señora came back with a tray bearing a Sèvres chocolate pot and two cups, another gift from The Corsair. She settled herself on the sofa with Rosie, poured out the chocolate and took a sip. She laughed. "I can never wait. I always burn my tongue, but that first hot sip is so good." She took a good look at Rosie. "*Dios, paloma.* What happened to you? You're dusty from head to hem.''

''Somebody came out of your gate and ran into me in the street. He knocked me flat and spilled everything in my basket.''

She laughed. ''Raider Lyons. He's usually in a better humor when he's spent the night here, but this morning he wasn't happy. He wants to sail with the first tide and several of his men are here, still asleep. I said I wouldn't disturb them, that they were the ones who had to remember their duty. He brags about what an excellent crew he has; they'll get where they need to be on time.''

''Raider Lyons? He told me his name is Robert. And what do you mean, his men?''

''I suppose his proper name is Robert. He's always been called Raider. And his men are the crew of his vessel. He's captain of the schooner *Avenger.*''

''Captain? He doesn't look much older than me. Are you sure?''

La Señora laughed her rich laugh once again and tugged at the bodice of her gown. ''*Paloma,* you have to fix this for me. It's gotten too snug somehow.''

Rosie knew how. Too much chocolate, too many sweets. ''I can take it with me. I brought the dresses I've been working on. I meant just to leave them. I didn't think anyone would be up so early.'' She pulled herself back to the question she'd asked before. ''Are you sure he's the captain of a ship?''

''Yes, yes, of course I'm sure. He must be twenty or so, certainly old enough to captain his own fighting ship and to act as a privateer for the American government. Has he never come to the Drop Anchor, he and his frightful friend, Nicodemus McNair?''

''I think I'd remember if he had,'' Rosie said, knowing for certain she would. "Who's Nicodemus McNair?"

"Him you would definitely remember," La Señora said, pouring herself more chocolate. "He is big as a house and has a fierce head of black hair and a black beard. There's a saber scar across his face and where it ends, in his scalp and in his beard, the hair is white. He rarely speaks, and it is said that he hates everybody but Raider."

"What's so special about Raider?" Rosie asked, finally drinking the chocolate she'd prudently allowed to cool.

La Señora languidly shrugged her ample white shoulders. "It is said that they have saved each other's lives, but I don't know. You know how all this war talk bores me. We in Campeche are neutral. I don't want to think of it. Let the English and the Americans be the ones who are bothered."

La Señora yawned and stood up. "Now, *paloma,* I must go to bed. I've been up all night. I'll send Miguelito to fetch you for the alterations when the girls have tried on their dresses. You can fix this dress then, too." She yawned again and then turned at the sound of bare feet running on tile. Through the arched doorway of the parlor, Rosie and La Señora watched six barefoot young men run past. They wore white sailors' pants and struggled to pull on their shirts as they ran, shoes in hands, through the front door.

La Señora began to laugh as the courtyard gate clanged closed. "Raider's crew on the way to sailing on the first tide. I told him." Still laughing, she moved majestically down the dim hallway, leaving Rosie to finish her chocolate alone.

Chapter 2

On her way back to the Drop Anchor, swinging her almost empty basket, Rosie wished she had time to go to the beach to gather shells. She used them on the gowns and blouses and skirts she made, embroidering fantastical sea creatures and seascapes embellished with real shells and bits of ocean-polished glass. She used only shells that had been abandoned; never would she evict a creature to take its shell.

What was a shell, after all, but a home? And home was a concept that was often in her mind. Though she'd lived above the Drop Anchor for twelve years, she didn't consider it a home. And her memories of the home she'd had in England before her mother died were hazy fragments: the corner of a garden where a sundial, green with age, stood useless in a blowing fog; a warm, dark room in which she lay on a cot, hearing the sounds but not the words of an argument; a small, plain woman sewing by a window, a silver thimble winking on her finger.

Rosie knew the woman at the window wasn't her mother. Her mother, as evidenced by the miniature in the locket that was her only legacy to Rosie, had been beautiful, with a sweet oval face and delicate, almost frail, features. Her hair had been thick and black, like Rosie's, but dressed elaborately atop her small head in a fashion Rosie could never have mastered, even with the help of La Señora and her girls. The locket was beautiful, too: silver with the image of a deer on it, a deer with a gold apple on a chain around its neck.

Most probably the woman she remembered was her Aunt Polly, her father's sister, with whom they had lived until her mother died, and who always ended her annual letter to Rosie's father with, "And a kiss for dear little Rosie."

Campeche would never be home, not the way she meant for home to be. How could a place whose name meant Place of Snakes and Ticks ever be home? The fact that her father, Percy Fielding, had accidentally come into ownership of the Drop Anchor was the only thing that had kept them in Campeche as long as they had been, and even so, Percy was always threatening to move on.

Rosie knew they wouldn't, not now, after all this time. Laziness was what had brought them to the Drop Anchor, the only cantina outside the walls of Campeche, where Percy was offered a job and sleeping rooms upstairs by the owner, another displaced Englishman. The offer of the rooms had saved Percy the trouble of looking for something better and, lazy as always, he had taken it. Just when he was getting itchy feet again, the Drop Anchor's owner had been knifed to death in one of the brawls he loved to incite, and with his last breath he had given the Drop Anchor, then called the Bitter End, to Percy.

Rosie suspected it was delirium from blood loss that had prompted him to do it, but many witnesses had sworn it was a legitimate legacy. For a while, Percy had enjoyed being the cantina's proprietor. He presided over the bar, the most handsome thing in the place, made from the mahogany paneling of a wrecked French merchantman, and hired a succession of serving girls who always quit when they found out that what he really wanted was for them to do all the work.

Then, when Rosie was twelve, Percy put her to work, saving himself the inconvenience of ever having to look for another hired girl.

Because the only home she could really remember consisted of the small, splintery rooms over the bar, was it any wonder that she would be fascinated by the tidy, pearly shell-homes she found washed up along the tide line of beaches that faced out to sea—and to where she hoped her future lay?

Her blouse was stuck to her shoulder blades before she'd gotten to the Puerta del Mar, the gate in the eight-foot-thick city wall leading to the harbor, and she wished she'd brought a hat to keep the sun out of her eyes. She passed through the portal and could see ships swinging languidly at anchor at the docks; farther out, other anchored ships rose and fell on the gentle Gulf swells. Shading her eyes, she studied the vessels on the swimming gold sea and wondered which one belonged to Captain Raider Lyons.

She shook her head, impatient with herself. What did it matter which ship was his? Her concerns at the moment consisted of scrubbing out the Drop Anchor's spittoons and laying in new supplies of Jamaican rum, English ale and *x-tabentum*.

As she approached the harbor, the noise of the log-wood loading almost caused her to miss the small sounds coming from a dry and stunted dust-gray bush by the side of the path. Bending to investigate, Rosie found the body of a dead mother cat curved around three dead kittens. She knew they were dead by the flies that had settled on them and which flew off in an annoyed swarm when Rosie knelt.

Tears came into her eyes and she silently affirmed the plan she had for herself when she got away from Campeche: she was going to adopt as many orphans, children and animals both, as she could and give them the kind of rambunctious, warm, loving home she wished she'd had.

When once she'd told this plan to La Señora, the woman had laughed her rich laugh and said, "Why not find a husband and make your own children?"

"I don't want a husband," Rosie had said. "From what I've seen of men, they're all either fools or cads or criminals. As long as I can support myself and my children, I can't think why I would want to put up with the posturing, the abuse, the drink and betrayal and neglect I've seen the women of Campeche tolerate." She hadn't said so, but even La Señora's girls, whose men weren't anywhere near permanent, had tolerated such treatment.

Rosie lightly touched the mother cat and each of the still kittens. As her hand brushed the last kitten, it opened its mouth, uttering the tiny peeping cry she had first heard over the noise from the harbor. Weakly, it bumped its fuzzy head against its mother's stomach.

Rosie scooped the kitten into her hand and stood. "Oh, poor baby. How long have you been here in this sun? We've got to get you something to eat, don't we?"

She definitely didn't have time for an extra errand, but how could she let this tiny creature starve?

It was more than half an hour later before she returned to the Drop Anchor, an *olla* of goat's milk in her basket and a squirming, crying kitten clutched against her chest. She kicked open the back door and was barely able to find a saucer, fill it with milk and present it to the kitten without being pricked to shreds by his tiny claws. Eagerly the kitten pushed his little face into the saucer, then raised his head, milk dripping from his whiskers, a puzzled expression on his face. He tried again with the same result and again looked bewildered before he began to cry once more.

This kitten was still too little to be away from his mother, Rosie could see that, but there was no help for it. If he wanted to survive, he would have to learn fast. She dipped her finger into the milk and put it into his mouth. The kitten sucked the milk off her finger and mewed pitifully when it was gone. She repeated the action over and over, until they were both tired of it. Wearily the kitten lowered his face into the saucer, and she could almost see his little brain trying to determine how to get more milk into himself faster. As she watched, he experimented with different lapping techniques until finally he found one that worked. That settled, he set to the serious work of filling himself up.

"Oh, how smart you are!" Rosie exclaimed. "And how determined. You and I are going to be wonderful friends."

She was sitting on the stained wood floor behind the bar, her skirt wadded around her, watching the kitten drink his milk, when her father came in the back door.

"What's that you've got there?" he asked, standing over her with a scowl on her face.

"It's a kitten, of course," she said. "His mother's dead and I've adopted him."

"One thing we don't need around here is another hungry mouth," Percy Fielding began.

"I'm the one who worries about feeding the mouths we've got," Rosie said, cutting him off, "and I need this one. I don't suppose you brought any supplies with you from wherever you've been."

"Now, Rosie," he said in a wheedling tone, "you know I can't carry anything, not with my chest so weak." He coughed experimentally. "Just this little er-

12

rand has wore me out. I'll be going upstairs now for a bit of a rest, I think.''

"You're supposed to be doing the sweeping up," she said, but she knew it was useless. It always was. She didn't know why she kept trying.

"Aw, Rosie," he said, already starting up the stairs. "What help will I be to you if I'm laid out on my deathbed?" He increased the speed of his getaway, so that he was more than halfway up the staircase before he finished what he was saying.

"What help is he to me now?" Rosie asked the kitten as Percy Fielding disappeared, to spend the afternoon in his singlet and drawers, sampling his own private stock of Jamaican rum.

Chapter 3

"What's wrong with you, Rosie?" Percy Fielding yelled across the bar as he shoved six slopping tankards of ale toward her. "You got your foot in a bucket?"

The Drop Anchor was full, the air thick with smoke and noise as seamen crowded the tables and stood around the walls, drinking, smoking Cuban cheroots or long clay pipes, laughing and singing in several languages. Already a few lay unconscious on the pile of sawdust in the corner. Around a table near the door sat the officers from the British frigate *Lightning* with their captain, Charles Lawrence.

Captain Lawrence was a regular customer of the Drop Anchor and, so far, the only man Rosie had been unable to fit into her categories of fool, cad or criminal. He was always gentlemanly and polite with her, for which she was surpassingly grateful. Most of the Drop Anchor's customers seemed to think she was there for their amusement as much as the alcohol was, and she'd gotten adept at avoiding their grasping hands.

Captain Lawrence's *Lightning* had been sailing the Caribbean and Mexican Gulf waters for the past five or six years, first as transport for the special envoy from

Jamaica to the British court; since January of 1812, when war was declared between the United States and England, he'd been on duty, searching for American privateers to blow out of the waters. The *Lightning* and *Lawrence* had been quite successful as privateer hunters in spite of the fact that the privateers that remained under sail this late in the war were the fastest, craftiest, most cunning vessels afloat, and the *Lightning* was too big to have their speed and maneuverability.

Part of his success, it was said, lay in a willingness to use tricks—the flying of false national flags, simulated distress, running up a white flag of spurious surrender during battle. Rosie had heard sailors talk in the Drop Anchor about these tactics, sometimes with admiration, sometimes with scorn. They were most universal in deploring his practice of sinking captured privateers with all hands aboard after removing everything of value.

Naturally, Rosie didn't like the sound of this, but war was war, wasn't it? Wasn't that Captain Lawrence's job, to stop the privateers? She wasn't sure where her loyalties lay in this war. She *was* half English. But she also lived in a neutral port where sailing men of all nations could come in safety, regardless of the many fights between seamen who apparently didn't understand the fine points of neutrality.

As she turned from the bar with her tray of drinks, she saw, through the smoky lantern light, Raider Lyons come in the open door of the Drop Anchor. With him was the most fearsome-looking man she'd ever seen— taller even than Raider and broader, with an aura of savage power. His face was distorted by a scar that ran diagonally across it, cutting from the hairline over his left eye, splitting the eyebrow, missing the eye but bisecting the nose and disappearing into his beard on the right cheek. His hair and beard were thick and black except where the ends of the scar touched. At those points, white streaks interrupted the black.

"Rosie!" her father shouted. "Move!"

Rosie blinked, then moved away from the bar with her tray of drinks. The noise level in the Drop Anchor diminished as head after head turned to watch Raider and the bearded man enter. A path opened for them when they started across the room as sailors unconsciously got out of their way.

The bearded man stopped before a small table where two men in the white trousers and short blue jackets of the English navy were obliviously throwing dice. One man looked up at Nicodemus McNair while the dice-thrower gathered the dice for another toss.

"Looks like I've got you now, Jake," the thrower said, shaking the dice in his fist. "I figure you owe me—" He looked up, too, finally aware of the quiet that had gathered around their table. The dice dropped from his fingers and clattered on the table. "Uh—" he said, startled speechless at the sight of the hulking brute staring down at him.

McNair grasped the back of Jake's chair and gave it a negligent shake—a shake which dislodged Jake onto the floor. Jake's gambling partner stood up so suddenly that his chair fell over backward, and he stepped around the table, away from Raider Lyons and Nicodemus McNair, his hands raised, palms out. "It's yours," he said hoarsely.

"Thank you." The bearded man's words were calm and quiet, unexpectedly refined, thick with the burr of Scotland.

Jake scrambled up from his place on the floor and skittered away into the crowd as the bearded man lowered himself into the chair he had continued to hold. He gestured to Raider, who bent and upended the fallen chair. Then he, too, sat and swept the room with an appraising glance. When it touched the table where Captain Charles Lawrence sat, he inclined his head and said, "Captain Lawrence." His voice was as full of hostility as a sharpened cutlass.

Charles Lawrence nodded. "Captain Lyons." Their voices, equal in animosity, were clear in the subdued cantina. Then Lawrence nodded to the bearded man. "McNair." The word rang with contempt.

The bearded man gave no indication he had heard. Instead, he turned to Rosie. "Rum," he said.

Criminal, she thought, cataloging him. No question about it. And Raider looked decidedly more criminal just now than he had this morning, when she had thought him a fool.

"Rum!" Nicodemus McNair roared, and Rosie flinched, spilling every tankard on her tray. Quickly she delivered the dripping tankards to the table that had ordered them, grateful that the men there were too interested in Nicodemus McNair to notice that their drinks weren't quite full.

By the time she reached the bar, Percy already had a bottle and two glasses on a tray, which he shoved across the mahogany surface. "Be quick," he said. "We don't want any trouble."

Rosie delivered the bottle and glasses, making it a point to look directly into the eyes of both Raider and Nicodemus McNair. Raider looked at her as if he'd never seen her before, and Nicodemus McNair's eyes were so black and shadowed she had the sense he wasn't seeing her at all. Suddenly she wanted to be upstairs cuddling her kitten, who had already learned to use the sandbox she had rigged for him and who was, when she'd come downstairs to work, asleep on her pillow, his little stomach warm and full of goat's milk.

∽∾∽

Chapter 4

As time passed, the men in the Drop Anchor got drunker and noisier. Rosie's eyes and throat burned from the pipe and cigar smoke. Her feet hurt. She's been up since sunrise and she was tired. She wanted this to be one night without a fight, without bloodstains to scrub up the next morning, one night when the Drop Anchor would close on time and every one would leave, mellow and satisfied.

She glanced at the table where Raider and Nicodemus McNair sat. They talked intently, their heads close together, their eyes moving constantly around the room in the habit of men accustomed to anticipating emergency. Raider's intelligent, gold-flecked glance passed over her as if she were furniture. She was annoyed with herself that this chafed her.

She hoisted another tray of *x-tabentum* for a table of men who were tasting it for the first time that evening. The initial experience of drinking it was unpredictable—some passed out almost immediately; others became ill or argumentative or amorous or violent—so she approached their table warily, distracting herself by imagining the excruciating headaches they would all have the next morning.

After Rosie had unloaded the drinks onto the table, one of the sailors, a thin man with a long, drooping mustache, snagged her around the waist with one hard arm and pulled her against him. Startled, she dropped the tray with a clatter that went unheard in the general din.

"You can keep me company for a bit," he said, trying to drag her onto his lap. "I've a trick or two I'd like to teach you."

Rosie pushed against his shoulders with all her strength, but she might as well have been pushing a wall. Most seamen were sinewy to begin with, and *x-tabentum* made them behave as if they were invincible.

"Take your hands off me," she cried, boxing his ear with one fist and pulling his hair with the other. He only laughed and dragged her closer. She twisted in his grip and said some of those words she wasn't supposed to know, but he kept laughing. His tablemates laughed, too, and one of them banged his fist gleefully on the table as Rosie struggled.

She was almost gagging at the smell of alcohol on the sailor's breath, and of his unwashed body. She never understood why so many sailors smelled so bad when they spent most of their time surrounded by water.

Now he had both her wrists held behind her in one large hand, his grip so tight her fingers were tingling with numbness. His wet and open mouth pressed into her cheek, and for the first time, she was frightened. She couldn't expect any help from the customers, most of whom would probably do the same thing to her given the opportunity, but why wasn't her father paying any attention? Why wasn't he, for once, acting like a proper father?

Suddenly there was silence at the table, and the sailor's hands withdrew from her waist and her wrists so quickly, she would have fallen had not a hand caught her neatly beneath the elbow and steadied her.

Confused, she looked up into the set face of Captain

Raider Lyons. Without looking at her, his attention still on the tableful of silent sailors, he drew her protectively closer to him, holding her lightly against his chest. As her cheek made contact with the clean white linen of his shirt, and with the warm plane of his chest beneath it, her whole body became alert.

"Well, girls," Raider said mockingly to the sailors. "Nothing better to do than terrorize a child?"

She was about to protest that she wasn't a child, but immediately thought better of it, and kept her silence. She could feel the beat of Raider's heart, slow and even, in her cheekbones, while her own bumped rapidly against the cage of her ribs. In front of her eyes were the burnished hairs of his chest in the open throat of his shirt, and her nose gave her evidence that he, unlike so many others, had bathed; she could smell soap and the leather of his vest and something else, clean and brisk, that might be just the scent of his skin.

"I wasn't annoying her," the evil-smelling sailor muttered, *x-tabentum* making him bold. "And any man with eyes in his head can see that she may be small, but she ain't no child."

The quiet around the table was spreading to the rest of the room as the other customers became interested in the drama. Past Raider's chest, Rosie could see faces turning in her direction, a few men getting to their feet for a better look.

Rosie's attacker stood now, too, facing Raider. "I wasn't doing nothing to you. Let her mind her own business. She's no princess who needs a rescue. What kind of woman do you think works in a place like this, anyway?"

His tablemates watched him silently, wise enough, or not yet drunk enough, to argue with someone who had Nicodemus McNair for a friend.

Raider released Rosie and looked down at her. "I

beg your pardon," he said. "Just tell me you wish to continue and I'll leave the two of you alone."

"Continue?" Rosie said. "I didn't even want to start."

Raider smiled and suddenly looked boyish, like someone Rosie really could believe was twenty, instead of the large, imposing avenger he had seemed a moment before. With a trace of the smile still on his mouth, he turned back to Rosie's attacker. "I believe you have your answer," he said.

"So you think it's funny," the sailor said, drawing his fists up in front of himself. "It was none of your business in the first place."

"Bosun," a new voice said, "I think not."

Rosie saw that Captain Charles Lawrence had come to stand beside Raider, who turned and said coldly, "Captain Lawrence. How unexpected to find the two of us in agreement on anything."

With Raider's head turned, the pugnacious sailor had drawn back his arm. Though one of his tablemates reached to restrain him, he missed, and the sailor landed a punch on Raider's shoulder just as Raider finished speaking. The blow caught Raider unprepared and he took a step backward, knocking into another table and upsetting the drinks there. The seamen at that table jumped to their feet, ale in their laps, ready to fight.

Before Rosie knew how it had come about, the entire Drop Anchor exploded into a riot. The speed and enthusiasm with which the men in the cantina entered the brawl affirmed her opinion that they came there *hoping* for a fight. As if the war at sea most of them were engaged in weren't enough, she thought, crawling under the table for protection. She found herself in a puddle of *x-tabentum,* and the fumes from it were enough to make her light-headed. What was it about men that made them love battle so? she wondered, considering that maybe *all* men were fools. Even her father, who

21

avoided participating directly in fights, had levered himself up to stand on the bar, where he could have the best possible view of the proceedings.

Raider was bent backward over a table by a man too drunk to fight but too heavy to get out from under, when the bosun who had started all the trouble approached him, holding an exotic-looking dagger with a curved blade. He raised it over his head and aimed for Raider's throat.

Rosie screamed his name, but he didn't hear.

Nicodemus McNair had sat quietly at his table drinking his rum as the fighting surged around him, no one quite decks-awash enough or foolhardy enough to approach him. He came instantly to his feet when he, too, saw the knife appear over the battling heads. He was too far from Raider to reach him through the throng, but he bellowed, "Raider! Look up!"

This voice Raider heard, and with a flexure of his powerful shoulders and arms, seasoned from long hours at a ship's wheel, he managed to push the heavy drunk off himself. The man slid to the floor, tipping the table and catapulting Raider to a standing position as the dagger started down. In a reflex motion, Raider twisted aside, pulled a small pistol from his waistband and fired once, a warning shot, high and to the right of the sailor, as with his other hand he grabbed the bosun's wrist and gave it one hard shake, causing the knife to drop to the floor. Then Raider hit the man across the face with the pistol and he fell, bleeding, at Raider's feet.

Only Rosie saw her father, still standing on the ornate mahogany bar, put his hand to his chest and fall backward the instant after the pistol had fired.

"Papa!" she cried, trying to get out from under the table. In her haste, she cracked her head on its underside and sat down again, dazed, in the puddle of *x-tabentum*.

The fighting tapered off quickly after the sound of

the shot as seamen, muddled by drink and fractiousness, recovered themselves. One unruly sailor in the corner by the sawdust pile continued, for the sheer animal pleasure of it, to pummel a man already hanging unconscious over his shoulder. As he drew back his arm for one final punch, his forearm struck the lamp in its hanging bracket and it dislodged, toppling onto the sawdust.

Instantly the sawdust pile blazed into peaks of flame. The Drop Anchor was old and dry, its timbers soaked in spirits: no better fuel for a fire could have existed.

No one made any effort to extinguish the blaze. Even the more willing could see that it would be futile. Instead, they made for the two doors, dragging with them their shipmates who were too decks-awash or too battered to make a retreat under their own power. The thicket of running legs was so dense around the table under which Rosie crouched that she couldn't force her way out. All she could think of was her father, fallen behind the bar. And the kitten, helpless upstairs.

Flames licked around the edges of the room and were making forays across the floor before Rosie could get out from under the table. The heat from the fire was intense against her flushed skin, and the smoke was so thick she could hardly see. Her eyes ran and her throat was seared by the heavy, acrid plumes. Coughing and wiping her streaming eyes with the backs of her hands, she fumbled her way toward the bar and her father. He hadn't been much of a father, but no one deserved to die like this, in this inferno.

Before she had taken more than a few steps, she felt hands on her shoulders, pulling her backward. "No!" she cried. "My father!"

"Nicodemus!" Raider called from behind her. "Find the old man and get him out! And you," he shouted to Rosie, pulling at her, "let's go! This place won't last more than a few minutes."

23

She struggled in his grasp. "I have to get my kitten! And my locket." Only as she said it did she realize how little she had that she valued enough to save.

"Forget them. Your life's worth more." His hands dragged her in the direction of the door, though she could see almost nothing. She couldn't believe the noise created by the fire; the crack of flames devouring dry wood was all around her, punctuated by detonations as overheated bottles of spirits broke, causing fresh, flaring towers to leap to the ceiling. The stench of rotted wood permeated with salt and sweat and burning alcohol filled Rosie's head, nauseating her. She fought against Raider, but he continued to pull her to the door.

To their right a beam fell, and the resulting explosive shower of sparks and noise gave her the unguarded moment she needed to break away from him and stumble toward the stairs she wasn't sure still existed. The heated smoke was too thick to see through, but she fought her way, dodging bursts of flame. Her hand, stretched before her in the noisy, searing gloom, encountered the rail of the staircase. She started up.

Halfway up the steps, an arm grabbed her around the waist. "If you have a death wish," Raider shouted into the roar of the conflagration, "there are easier ways."

Rosie had had more than enough of men manhandling her. "Leave me alone!" she screamed, ripping herself away from him and running up the rest of the stairs. The smoke was somewhat less heavy here, and she could see the outline of her closed bedroom door. She pushed it open, and Raider came in with her, slamming it behind them.

"What is it you want?" he asked. "Be quick."

"Stop telling me what to do," she snapped, yanking open the drawer in her washstand. She pulled out her mother's locket and opened it. In the side opposite her mother's picture was a tiny key embedded in wax, softened now from the heat of the fire. She didn't know what the key opened, but it had meant something to her mother and she wasn't going to lose it. She pressed the key firmly into the wax and closed the locket.

"What else?" Raider yelled above the noise of the flames.

Rosie scooped up the kitten from where he cowered, crying, against her pillow. "Baby, baby," she murmured, cuddling him against her chest. "It's all right—everything's going to be all right." She repeated the same words mothers have always said to their children, often with no more reason than she had to believe the truth of them. Had anyone ever said them to her? She couldn't remember.

"What else?" he asked again.

She hesitated for a moment, looking at the coverlet on her bed. It had taken her a year to embroider, an underwater garden of fantasy plants and rock formations and swimming creatures. The real shells in the pattern were woven over with green-and-gold-yarn seaweeds, and there were broken bits of amber-colored shells for her sea creatures' eyes and undersea flowers edged with sparkling chips of sea glass. She whisked it off the bed and wadded it into her arms around the kitten. "Nothing. Let's get out of here."

She opened the door into an eruption of flame from below, and the crashing sound of the staircase falling in on itself vibrated through the torrid air.

Raider hit the door with his palm and slammed it shut in their faces. "We're not leaving that way." He made a quick study of the small room. "There's only one other way." He stepped to the widow. "And this is it."

Rosie stood next to him, hugging the kitten so tightly he cried in protest, and looked down. She remembered all the times she'd sat in this room, sewing, looking out the window and wishing she could fly away with the gulls, away from Campeche, on to her own life. Now she looked down at the dark sand lit by lurid flames and said faintly, "I don't know . . ."

"Give me the cat," he said. Rosie loosened her grip on the kitten and Raider lifted him in one big hand, depositing him in the pocket of his leather vest. Then he took the locket from her clenched fist and put it in with the cat. "You won't have to jump, Nettle," he said quietly. "I'll help you. Get ready."

She wrapped the coverlet around her shoulders and tied it clumsily in front. Going out that window looked like a leap into Hell. But at the edge of her vision, a white frill of waves from the Gulf unfurled onto the sand, cool, clean and sibilant.

"What should I do?" she asked.

"I'm going to lower you through the window. I won't drop you. I'll let you down as easily as I can. Sit on the windowsill and give me your hands."

She did as he told her. The touch of his hands on her wrists was as hot as the air she breathed. Gradually, he eased her over the sill, his grip tight and strong, until she was dangling along the front of the building. She could feel hot, crackling wood all down the front of her, could sense the fire barely contained.

"I'm going to let you go now."

Something in his calm voice gave her confidence.

"I'm ready."

"When you hit the ground, run away from the building, down the beach. I'll be right behind you. Now!"

As he released her, she heard the percussive sound of her bedroom door being blown in by the force of the blaze. She fell with a thump onto the sand. Before she could assess any damage to herself, Raider landed lightly beside her, yanked her upright so forcefully she thought her shoulders had been dislocated and dragged her with him down the beach. When they were safely away from the fire, he threw her to the sand and rolled on top of her.

26

Chapter 5

"Stop it! Stop! What are you doing? Get off me!"
This constant mauling by anybody who came along was getting tiresome, Rosie thought as she squirmed under Raider's large, heavy body. Besides, the kitten was in his pocket and she couldn't imagine what all this rolling around was doing to him.

"Quiet," Raider said, lying full length on her, pressing her into the damp sand. "I'm trying to put out the fire."

"But the fire's back there," she gasped, the air squeezed from her lungs by his weight. "I don't know how this is going to help."

He laughed in her ear. "Your dress is on fire, Nettle," he said. "But I think it's out now." He slid off her and sat in the sand, inspecting her.

"Oh," she said, pushing herself into a sitting position. "Am I hurt?"

"Both legs are burned," he said, and she felt his palm skim her scorched flesh. She yanked her legs away from him, noting that somehow she'd lost her shoes and that most of her skirt below the knees was burned away. "As far as I can tell, that's all, but apparently you don't want me to make a more thorough examination."

"I definitely do not," she said. With light only from

the moon and the dim flickers from the fire, she couldn't see her injuries well enough to know how badly she was hurt. "How odd. I must be burned—look at my dress—but I don't feel any pain."

"The same thing happens in battle," he said matter-of-factly. "I've had wounds I never remembered getting."

"My father," she said, suddenly remembering. "You shot my father."

He rose, standing between her and the moon, so that he was nothing but a large, ominous shadow. "Did I?" he asked.

"When you fired your pistol in there. Your bullet hit my father." Surprisingly, her voice quavered. It wasn't only her father she had lost, small loss that he was; it was her home, her livelihood and almost everything she possessed.

"I'll go see what Nic has done with him. Stay here. I don't want to have to save you from anything more."

"No one asked you to save me to begin with," she told him indignantly. First he had started the fight that caused the Drop Anchor to burn, then he had shot her father, and now he was annoyed with her for needing saving. Really, he was outrageous.

He turned and strode up the beach, back toward the Drop Anchor, his tall silhouette outlined by the remaining glow from the fire.

Rosie sat on the damp sand, aware now of the pain from her burned legs. Her eyes filled with tears. Through the shimmer of them, she could see the last timbers of the building fall inward with a swirl and shower of sparks.

Raider Lyons, the man she held responsible for everything that had happened, had just walked away into the darkness with the only two things remaining to her.

Rosie sobbed, taking great shuddering gasps of air and then weeping some more. After a few minutes, she

28

took a deep breath and quit crying. She was a practical person and she knew that no matter how long she cried, eventually she'd have to get up, determine what had happened to her father, tend to her burns and find a place to sleep for the rest of the night. She wiped her face on her sleeve, leaving big sooty smudges. Well, her dress was ruined anyway, and it didn't matter how many hours she'd spent embroidering the flowers around the neckline and the hem that wasn't there anymore.

Painfully, she got to her feet. Her burned legs hurt now, and she was shivering, though the night was warm. She could smell the smoke in her hair, and she felt gritty and dirty all over. Limping to the water's edge, she tried to wash her hands in the bay. Salt water without soap made an ineffective combination, and she gave up, reluctantly drying her filthy hands on her coverlet.

Perhaps she could go to La Señora's. There were plenty of beds there, though at this hour of the night they would probably all be in use. Maybe she could even stay there, working for La Señora and her girls, cleaning or sewing or cooking—anything but what the girls did.

But first she had to find out what had happened to her father.

As she started up the beach, she saw two tall shadows headed in her direction. They could be anybody—drunken sailors, the bosun with the wicked knife, anybody.

There was no place to hide. The beach was wide and white and the crescent moon hung in the sky, illuminating her.

She turned and ran, the coverlet tied around her shoulders flapping awkwardly.

And immediately she heard running footsteps in the sand behind her, footsteps that quickly caught up with her. Arms circled her from behind, pinning her against a hard male body. She twisted and squirmed and yelled, but it was useless.

"Nettle," Raider's voice said from behind her, "it's only me. I thought you were going to wait for word of your father."

She quit struggling. There was an odd sort of comfort in resting in his arms, in leaning back against him; an illusion of having someone she could depend upon, someone to help her with her burdens. But if there was such a person, Raider Lyons wasn't it.

She straightened her spine and stepped out of his grasp. "My father," she said, shivering, rubbing her arms. "Did you find him?"

"Nic," he called, motioning with his arm.

The other tall shadow materialized into Nicodemus McNair. "I got him out o' the fire, but he was already dead." He shrugged his massive shoulders. From the tone of his voice, it was clear he didn't care in the slightest that his rescue hadn't been in time.

She couldn't stop shivering.

"What will you do now?" Raider asked her. "Those burns need treatment."

Where would she go now? La Señora's? The church? She hadn't been there since Father Xavier went to Mérida.

"Then you'll have to come with us," Raider said, interrupting her long silence.

"What?" How could he make such a bizarre suggestion? She'd rather sit here on this beach forever than go anywhere with him, no matter how good he looked or smelled or felt. He was a privateer at war, and he had friends as fearsome as Nicodemus McNair. Sitting on this beach forever would probably be the wiser, and the safer, choice.

"Raider," Nicodemus said, warning in his voice. "Leave it be."

"I know what I'm doing, Nic. You know I don't like to leave my affairs unfinished."

"This is nay your affair," Nicodemus McNair said. "Leave it be."

"How can you say it's not my affair when I've shot her father? We can take her to Octavia. She needs a *traiteur* for her burns. I won't leave her here to be treated by that same charlatan who let Rob Hendry bleed to death from a wound a *traiteur* could have mended in a day."

"Who's Octavia?" Rosie asked. "What can a traitor do for a burn? I want to stay right here." Campeche, the place she had always wanted to leave, suddenly took on several shades of enchantment.

"I've got your cat in my pocket," Raider said to her, "and it's going with me. Whether you do or not is up to you."

She dived for his pocket, but he caught her hands before she made contact. "Somehow I guessed you'd try that," he said. "We're going now." Still holding both her hands, he started along the beach, pulling her with him.

"Why should I have to go to a traitor?" she asked, struggling to keep up with him. "I'll be fine here. We have a doctor." She pushed from her mind poor Rob Hendry, whoever he was, bleeding to death. "What do you care what happens to me, anyway?" She'd seen him hit a man in the face with a pistol and shoot another man—admittedly, that was probably an accident, but still, it didn't seem to bother him—so why should he worry about her burns? "Why is a little kitten you didn't think important enough to save from a fire so important to you now?"

"I like to finish what I start," he said again.

As far as she was concerned, he'd already finished off everything that was important to her.

"Let her go," Nicodemus McNair said from behind her. For a man who, according to La Señora, rarely spoke, he was certainly doing a lot of talking about what Captain Lyons should be doing with her. "This is nay the way for you to exercise your overdeveloped sense of responsibility."

"I didn't think you'd be averse to the performance of a good deed, Nic," Raider said, continuing down the beach with Rosie stumbling beside him. "Hasn't it always been your contention that an element of such charity confers humanity on one's character? And wouldn't you agree that my character could stand the addition of some humanity?"

"I gave that up long ago," Nicodemus said. "And you know it. Now I believe only in self-preservation. And this good deed of yours could compromise that. The more connections, the more risk."

"I'm perfectly aware of that," Raider said, stopping where a boat was drawn up onto the sand.

The two men stood facing each other, the moon casting a demon light on both their faces: Nicodemus's so fierce, Raider's like stone. Finally McNair gave a faint shake of his head and bent to push the gig into the water.

Rosie knew it was beyond her capacity to negotiate her own release if someone like Nicodemus McNair had failed at it. Besides, her kitten and her locket were in Raider's pocket and she knew she had to go where they went. "After this traitor sees to my burns," she said a little breathlessly, "then you'll bring me back here, is that right?"

"Of course," Raider said, his voice calm and reasonable. He led her into the water, lifted her over the side of the gig and climbed in beside her. As McNair hauled on the oars, the dark walls of Campeche receded into the night.

Chapter 6

The salt water on her burns stung, and in spite of the balminess of the night air, she trembled.

Raider felt her trembling in his hands and moved so that he held both her hands firmly in one of his as he put his arm around her shoulders. She could feel his body heat even through the leather vest, but instead of warming her, it caused her to tremble even more.

"Can it be that you're afraid of me?" he murmured, his lips almost touching the top of her head. "Is that possible? Someone who ran straight into a fire for a kitten?"

Suddenly she was conscious of how she must smell, of smoke and sweat and spirits. She tried to pull away from him, but he drew her back.

"Why should I be afraid of you?" she asked, relieved that her voice sounded firm and strong.

"Should I tell her, Nic? About the bloodstains the war has left on my soul? That half my own crew think I've lost my reason? That four years searching could easily become a lifetime of futility? Should I?" His hold on Rosie tightened.

"Raider," McNair murmured, half warning, half censure.

"You sound like every man who comes into the Drop Anchor," Rosie said stoutly, ignoring her racing heart and the real fear that was growing in her. "They all want to sound as if they're the most dangerous characters on the high seas. If they'd done as much killing and sinking as they say, there wouldn't be a ship still afloat in the Gulf or the Caribbean, and probably not in the world. And not a single one of them would have gone into a fire with me to save my cat."

His grip on her relaxed infinitesimally. "You don't believe me?"

"I grew up on stories about the pirates who ransacked Campeche before the walls were built: William Parker and Diego the Mulatto; peg-legged Pata de Palo; Lorencillo, who stole everything, including women, from the city; and Lewis Scott; and El Olonés, who was mad and punished his victims by peeling all their skin off. Nobody can scare me the way they do, and they're all dead." Tales about these pirates were the only bedtime stories her father had ever told her, and often, after hearing them, she would lie awake for hours, panicky and alone, waiting for Campeche to again be invaded by pirates who would come first to the Drop Anchor, outside the protection of the city walls.

"That's difficult competition," Raider said.

"Besides," Rosie added reasonably, "La Señora told me you're a privateer, and whatever you've done, while it might be considered piracy in peacetime, is perfectly legitimate during a war." She would not allow him to frighten her with his insinuations.

Nicodemus McNair pulled on the oars and gave her a look that, despite the distortion of his scars, seemed to be speculative, though she couldn't guess what he was speculating.

"Oh, yes," Raider said. "Letters of marque and reprisal from the American government excuse everything

I've done." His laugh was harsh. Then his voice lightened. "I see that I can't impress her, Nic, the way I do all the others. Quite a blow to my vanity. Shall I feed her to the fishes?"

Before Nicodemus could answer, the gig bumped lightly against the side of a ship that Rosie could barely see in the dark.

Immediately a deep male voice with a foreign cadence to it called down to them. "Who is it?"

"Baptiste? It's Raider. I'm coming aboard with a surprise for Octavia. And get Tuti up. I have a patient for her."

A rope ladder snaked over the side and fell with a thump into the gig, barely missing Rosie's head.

"Wait here," Raider said to McNair. "I'll deliver her and be right back." He stood, pulling Rosie up with him.

Be right back? Rosie thought. Wasn't this his ship? Did he mean to leave her on someone else's ship?

She was so cold and so apprehensive she could hardly stand in the heaving boat, but she refused to give him the satisfaction of seeing that. Bracing her feet for balance, she stood straight, clutching her grimy coverlet around her for warmth and courage.

Raider gave her a shove toward the ladder. "You first. I'll be right behind you, enjoying the view."

The amusement—or perhaps cruelty—in his voice moderated her fear with indignation. She didn't find the prospect of his looking under her skirt as she hauled herself up the ladder, and treating her discomfort so casually, the least bit entertaining. Of course, if he actually had done the awful things he wanted her to believe he had, her discomfort would mean nothing to him. And neither would abandoning her to some other ship's captain who might be even more of a criminal than Raider.

She climbed fast, sped by the knowledge that Raider was right behind her. When she gained the head of the ladder, she was prompted to turn right around and go back down and would have, had not Raider's shoulder been crowding a portion of her anatomy that she would just as soon keep to herself.

Eager hands grabbed hers and yanked her over the gunwale, scraping her burned legs painfully.

"Careful," Raider ordered, too late, from behind her. "She's hurt."

She looked up directly into the face, illuminated by the deck lanterns, of a swarthy, grinning, bare-chested man, his short black curls bound by a strip of red cloth tied in a knot over one ear, an ear that held a large gold hoop.

"Oh, my," Rosie said faintly.

The dark man released her hands as Raider followed her onto the deck. He turned his big white smile in Raider's direction and held out his hand, which Raider shook. Then the swarthy man grabbed Raider in an embrace with his free arm and pounded him on the back.

It gave Rosie no comfort to see that they were such warm colleagues. Nor did it comfort her to see the way the mounded muscles on the dark man's chest and shoulders tightened as he moved.

"It's good to see you, Baptiste. Is Octavia up?" Raider asked.

"Aye. It's another of her wakeful nights."

Rosie might have found the exotic inflections of the dark man's speech pleasing if she'd met him under different circumstances. As it was, she found them only sinister.

"Well, perhaps this will distract her. And Tuti, too." Raider lounged against the gunwale, his long legs stretched in front of him, the heels of his hands resting on the sleek wood behind him as the barefoot man with the earring ran lightly across the deck and down through a hatchway. Other sailors moved about the deck, nodding or raising a hand in greeting to Raider.

Rosie looked toward the shore of Campeche; in the moonlight she could make out the dim outlines of docked ships riding at anchor. She was exhausted and frightened and in pain, but still, she assessed the distance between herself and the side of the ship, calculating how fast she could cover the distance, how long it would take her to swim to shore. She winced involuntarily at the thought of the salt water on her burns and decided it was probably just as well she didn't know how to swim.

"I wouldn't try it," Raider said softly. "I'd have you before you got anywhere near the rail."

She turned her back on him with all the dignity she could muster, adding a negligent little flounce for good measure, as if escape were the farthest thing from her mind.

As she watched, Baptiste emerged from the hatch. Behind him were two women. The first was as tall as Baptiste, slender and graceful in a seaman's trousers and striped shirt. Her face was a beautiful and serene oval, framed by long, loose waves of hair the color of the moonlight.

The other woman couldn't have been more different. She was shorter even than Rosie and twisted, with one shoulder higher than the other. Her face was wizened like a dried apple, and a kerchief covered her hair. Her long blue skirt didn't disguise the fact that her feet were bare. Most remarkable of all, she was smoking a small clay pipe, and the friendly aroma of good Cuban tobacco spiced the air.

Rosie hastily shut her mouth, which she hadn't recalled opening. If she'd been ordered at gunpoint to choose a side to jump to, she wouldn't have been able to decide between the perils of the three strangers approaching her or those represented by Raider Lyons. It wasn't likely, though, that she would be offered any say in the matter.

"Raider," said the tall blond woman, her voice as low and smooth as water over stone. "I sent a boat to the *Avenger* as soon as we anchored, but you'd already gone ashore."

"Octavia," he said, coming up to her and taking her in his arms. "I saw the *Ladyship* make anchor. I meant to come sooner, but circumstances intervened."

"How often they seem to do that with you," she said, pressing her cheek to his and closing her eyes. Raider held her, and as Rosie watched, every line of his long body relaxed. Why that should bother her, she couldn't begin to understand.

Raider drew back, still holding Octavia around the waist. Searching her face with his probing gaze, he asked, "Any news?"

She shook her head. "I saw Laffite at The Cove six weeks ago. He says Governor Claiborne has declared him an outlaw and offered a five-hundred-dollar reward for his capture. Laffite has offered five *thousand* dollars for Governor Claiborne."

Raider laughed, an easy, almost boyish sound that couldn't have surprised Rosie more than if he had taken flight.

"He took two English supply ships," Octavia continued. "Prunes and tea and a hogshead of opium. Not much of that left by now, I'll wager, but plenty of prunes and tea."

Raider laughed again, and with one arm still around Octavia's waist, he bent and embraced the small, gnarled woman. "Tuti," he said. "All is well with you?"

"To see you whole means all is well," she replied.

Rosie watched, amazed. Where had this gentle, laughing boy come from? Where was the man who had killed her father and then calmly cracked a sailor across the face with the murder weapon? Or the man who had tried to frighten her with the pure force of his personality?

She sensed attention on her and turned to find Baptiste watching her. Slowly he winked one of his dark, liquid eyes and grinned his great white smile at her. Quickly, she looked down at her grimy toes.

As she studied the smooth deck beneath her feet, she felt Raider's hand on her arm. "This girl—" he began, and paused. "Let me see if I can remember all those names you have." He wrinkled his brow. "Rosalba—"

"*Rosalia,*" she interrupted. "It's from my mother. She was Portuguese."

Everyone watched her in silence. Defiantly, she stared back.

"Forgive me," he said. "*Rosalia* Maria-Luisa Unity Fielding. Half English and, apparently, half Portuguese. Miss Fielding had the misfortune to be present at a tavern brawl that got out of hand. In the process, her father was killed and the tavern burned down. Unfortunately, the tavern was also her home. She has some nasty burns on her legs, so I brought her here for Tuti to treat. Then you can decide what you want to do with her."

Octavia was studying Raider with eyes the blue-green color of the sea and every bit as intelligent as his. "What is there to decide?" she asked. "I've got no place for her on the *Ladyship.*" She cast Rosie an acute, assessing glance and looked away again. Rosie felt as if she'd been measured and discarded. "What's your part in this, Raider?" Octavia asked.

"You sound like Nicodemus," Raider said, looking away from her. "I'm the one who killed her father."

His set face showed no emotion. "Treat her burns and put her ashore."

Rosie's shoulders sagged with relief. She was not to be abandoned to a shipful of cutthroats after all.

"Why don't you take Tuti aboard the *Avenger?*" Octavia asked. "You need her more than I do. The *Ladyship* is too fast to get into many fights. You, on the other hand, go looking for them."

Rosie was confused. Was Tuti the traitor? She'd thought it was Octavia. Who, then, *was* Octavia?

"Thank you, no," Raider said. "My men aren't as enlightened as yours. They won't have a woman on board as part of the crew. Women as passengers or plunder are another matter, of course. If we have need of Tuti's help, we'll put in at The Cove and wait for you."

"You won't wait long. I stay close, usually. I'm only here because I was chased in by *Lightning.* I could have eluded her, but I knew I'd be safe in a neutral port and perhaps I would find word of you. It was a boon to find *Avenger* in the harbor."

Raider took hold of Octavia's shoulders and looked into her face. "God, I wish this would end." She nodded and he pressed his lips to her forehead and then to each cheek as Rosie watched, round-eyed. Octavia rested her head against Raider's shoulder for a moment, then straightened, raising her chin.

"When do you sail?" she asked.

"In an hour. I'd meant to leave this morning, but couldn't get the water loaded aboard in time to catch the tide. Now I'm glad we waited."

"Be careful. Lawrence is always watching for you."

"And I him. Don't worry."

"You know how I hate to watch you sail," she said. "Godspeed." She turned and with quick steps crossed the deck, went down the hatch and disappeared from sight.

Raider turned to Tuti, embraced her again and said, "*Adieu,* Tuti."

He clapped Baptiste on the shoulder. "Stay ready."

Then he threw one long leg over the gunwale, looked at Rosie and drew it back. He came to stand before her. "If our paths cross again, Nettle, I hope it's under better circumstances. I regret your father's death."

A remote kindness lurked in his eyes, in contrast to the resolute toughness of his young face, and his dark brows were drawn together in—in what? Concern? Puzzlement? Severity? She couldn't tell.

She lifted her face, smudged with soot and streaked with tears, and said, with sincerity, "Thank you."

Gravely, he took a step closer to her. Then, taking her face into his hands, he leaned down and kissed her.

The warmth of his mouth on her cold lips was such a stunning surprise, such an explosive revelation, that Rosie had to grab handfuls of his linen shirtsleeves to keep herself from dropping straight to the deck of the *Ladyship.*

Even as she registered so many fresh and unique sensations, Raider ended the kiss. He paused for a moment, looking down into her face, and she could see the intelligence snapping like sparks in the depths of his hazel eyes. She was sure he could tell she had never before been kissed, as well as the effect his kiss had had on her, and she was mortified, for some unfathomable reason, by her lack of experience. She was further mortified by the thought that her breathing could probably be heard by the lookout at the top of the mainmast.

What she couldn't tell from the composed arrangement of Raider's deliberately expressionless face was the effect of the kiss on him.

As if to answer her, he lowered his mouth to hers

again. This time he drew her closer to him, and she clutched even more desperately at the material of his shirt.

Abruptly, he raised his head, breaking the kiss, and put her away from him.

She staggered a little, getting her balance, and then watched as he made a salute to those on the deck and flung himself over the gunwale, down the rope ladder, into the gig.

Chapter 7

It wasn't until Raider and Nicodemus McNair had rowed away from the *Ladyship* that Rosie recovered enough to remember her kitten. She ran to the vessel's stern and leaned over the taffrail, searching the dark water for the gig.

"You still have my cat!" she cried into the darkness.

Drifting over the black water with surprising clarity came a laugh. "Don't worry," Raider's voice said, "he's asleep in my pocket. We'll make a pirate of him."

Then the boom of Nicodemus McNair: "If we dinna make soup of him first."

"Soup?" Was he serious? She could believe almost anything of someone with a face like his. "Please!" she cried. "Bring him back! He's just a baby. He needs milk." The only answer Rosie got was the receding splash of oars.

Fighting tears and helpless fury, she stood at the railing. Being frightened to death amidst so many strangers with unknown intentions was bad enough even without the pain from her burned legs. Crowning everything, almost obscuring it, was her resentment at the blossoming of some turbulent new emotion learned in an instant in the arms of a young man who looked like a dream and behaved like a nightmare. A young man who was her father's killer.

What she didn't know was whether she would feel as she did now when *anyone* kissed her, or if it was only Raider Lyons who called forth such a reaction. Perhaps she should turn around and ask Baptiste to kiss her, just to find out. To do that made as much sense as anything else that had happened that night.

Oh, she'd been right in her lifelong distrust of men. They were nothing but trouble. She'd seen the misery men brought to La Señora's ladies. She'd watched them pine and curse, weep and rage over the men in their lives, and to no avail. Men went their own ways, without regard to what women wanted. They were selfish and domineering, vain and demanding. She'd never understood why the ladies couldn't keep their dealings with men on the level of simple commerce.

Until now.

It was a knowledge she didn't want.

She didn't know how long she might have stood, straight-backed, watching the roiling black water, pretending that there wasn't a shipful of who-knew-what behind her, if she hadn't felt a touch on her arm.

"Come," Tuti said. "Let me have a look at those burns."

She took Rosie's hand and led her across the empty deck. Rosie sighed heavily and followed, barely noting the gleam of the polished woodwork in the glint from the night lanterns, her shoulders slumping with the exhaustion of feigning bravery. Baptiste and the others had left so silently that Rosie hadn't heard them go.

Tuti started down the companionway under an open hatch, still holding Rosie's hand and tugging her along behind. The passageway at the foot of the steps was dim and close and smelled of warm wood and lamp oil—sleepy, safe smells.

Tuti opened a door and brought Rosie into her cabin. Here the smells were sharper; Rosie caught wintergreen and primrose and anise. Tuti pushed her into a straight wooden chair and went to light the lantern.

As Tuti turned up the flame, Rosie saw rows of shelves and cupboards fastened to the walls of the small space. The shelves, rimmed with railings, held ranks of green, corked jars. Swags of drying herbs hung from the low ceiling and lay in flat baskets on the floor. The only other furnishings in the room were a table, two chairs, one of which Rosie occupied, and a bunk. A spread of light brown cloth striped with blue covered the bunk. A border of hand-tied lace edged the spread, and tassels embellished the corners. Without thinking, Rosie stood and went to sit on the bed, where she stroked her hand across the soft bedcover, then fingered the fine lace.

"You like it?" Tuti asked. Her voice was resonant, like an alien musical instrument, with the same exotic lilt to it that Baptiste's had. "My mother made it. From *coton jaune*. Do you know French? No? That translates to yellow cotton, but it is known as brown cotton in Louisiana. I do not know why. One of the mysteries of our world. I do not try to understand them all anymore. I cannot."

Neither can I, Rosie thought.

She looked up to find Tuti standing before her, their eyes almost on a level. Tuti held a copper bowl in her hands. "The spread was part of my *L'Amour de Maman*."

"What's that?" Rosie asked. Determined not to cower, she studied Tuti's wizened face and was mollified to find only gentleness in it. If that's what traitors look like, she thought, it's no wonder they're so hard to recognize.

"It means, in French, 'Mother's love.' For Cajuns, *L'Amour de Maman* is the trousseau a mother makes for each of her children, the boys, too. She starts when the children are small, and by the time the weddings begin, there are blankets and sheets and spreads and table linens and pillows ready for the new houses.''

Mother's love. How could Rosie know what that meant? ''What's a Cajun?'' she asked.

''It's a long story about Cajuns. Sometime perhaps I will tell you, if you care to hear. Lie down now and let me look at these burns of yours Raider is so worried about.''

Obediently, Rosie lay down, finally depleted. Lying on Tuti's mattress was like being supported by a cloud, completely unlike the bed Rosie had slept on at the Drop Anchor, stuffed with straw, stiff and crackling and scratching her during the night.

''What's in this mattress?'' she asked.

''Spanish moss,'' Tuti answered, setting the bowl on the table. ''There is nothing better to sleep upon.''

She moved the lantern closer and bent over Rosie's legs. Her small, agile hands, warm and strong, slipped over Rosie's burns, somehow comforting and reassuring. Rosie nestled into the sweet-smelling brown coverlet and her eyelids felt weighted.

''I can fix this, no trouble,'' Tuti said.

''How?'' Rosie asked drowsily and only slightly suspiciously. ''What will you do?''

''First, wash with the juice of calendula flowers. Then a poultice of their leaves. Then a pad of cobwebs. I wish I had a fresh egg. The skin inside the shell is best. But for this burn, calendulas and cobwebs will have to do. It will be fine.''

Rosie heard the splash of liquid into the copper bowl and the clink of bottles being moved. Her eyes were so heavy she couldn't open them. Coolness moved over her burns and her last conscious thought was, I hope she doesn't poison me.

Chapter 8

Lulling motion, tangy air, downy warmth. Some infant memory stirred; she had felt this before, long ago. And now it was back, an unanticipated gift. Rosie lay, her eyes closed, savoring the moments, and chased after the wisps of a lullaby that flickered through her mind. A lullaby associated with warmth and sea smells and rocking.

It wouldn't come, was displaced by other sounds: creaking timbers, footsteps, the slap of rushing water on wood.

Rushing water!

She opened her eyes and sat up. She was in Tuti's bunk, the *coton jaune* coverlet over her, sunlight blasting through the square, rippled panes of the single window. In full light the cabin was not the place of fragrant secrets it had been the night before, but a cheerful workshop, the domain of someone whose work was woven into her life. If Rosie hadn't been so alarmed, she might have been able to appreciate it.

She leapt from the bunk and ran barefoot across the smooth wood floor, some wayward part of her mind comparing it to the splinters of the Drop Anchor, to the window. Spray flew against the panes in diamond darts as the *Ladyship* lifted and fell over the heave of the sea.

They were under sail!

She rushed to the door, still in her burned and crumpled dress. As her hand fell on the latch, the thought flitted through her mind that she might have soiled Tuti's snug bed with her dirty clothes, and she turned back to take a guilty look. Somehow, her own embroidered cover had been spread under her, so that Tuti's bed was protected, though Rosie's cover now appeared to be filthy beyond repair. The sight of her dirty hand on the latch made her think of how she had clutched, like some spineless ninny, the white sleeves of Raider's shirt when he had kissed her.

She hoped the shirt was as ruined as her bedcover.

She remembered her kitten aboard the *Avenger*, jerked the door open and ran down the passage to the companionway.

Standing at the top of the steps, she could hear the huge sails thumping tightly in the wind and its singing in the shrouds. Sailors were busy on the deck, winding coils of rope, mending sails, doing things up in the rigging that looked dangerous.

This shipboard life was a foreign world to Rosie, for as much time as she'd spent looking at the ships in Campeche's harbor, she had never been aboard one.

Sunlight bounced off the brass fittings and mellowed the polished wood of the deck to honey. White sails plumply filled with warm wind stood against a sky so bathed in blue that it hurt Rosie's eyes to look at it.

For so long she had stood on the shore in Campeche, looking out at the vast blue plate of ocean, feeling trapped and earthbound. Now she seemed to fly on the wings of the wind, and exhilaration caroled through every part of her.

Her long black hair whipped across her face, the

smell of smoke still in it; the smell of smoke reminding her that she was supposed to be ashore.

She almost wished she could stay.

Lowering her eyes from the sky and the sails, Rosie found the fascinated gaze of every man on deck focused upon her. Abashed, she took a quick step backward, down the steps, and backed into Tuti on the way up.

"I am sorry to startle you," Tuti said. "Between bare feet and the sounds of the ship, it is hard to hear someone approach."

"I was already startled when I woke up," Rosie said, turning to her. "I was supposed to be put ashore last night.""

"Oh, *oui*," Tuti said. "Octavia is impulsive sometimes. I am used to it. Best to accept what comes and try to enjoy it."

"But I can't stay here!" Rosie cried. "I have to go home." She disregarded, for the moment, that there was no home to go to. "I've got to see to the Drop Anchor, settle my father's affairs. And I have to get my kitten off the *Avenger*. You must turn around and let me get off."

Tuti laughed, a rough little chuckle. "We've been four hours at sea. Octavia will not turn around and perhaps run right into the *Lightning*. Captain Lawrence would love nothing better."

"What does Octavia have to do with it? I need to talk to the captain."

"But Octavia *is* the captain," Tuti told her.

"Octavia's the captain?" Rosie said, dumbfounded. She had never heard of a woman sea captain. "Not Baptiste?"

Tuti laughed her raspy little laugh. "Baptiste is quartermaster. Octavia is captain."

Wonderful, Rosie thought. Octavia, the most intimidating woman I've ever seen. Raider Lyons's woman.

She squared her shoulders. "I'll have to talk to Octavia, then. Where is she?"

"Would it do me any good to tell you you are wasting your time?" Tuti asked.

Rosie thought of her kitten. "No. I can't stay here. Where is she?"

Tuti shrugged. *"Eh bien."* She put her small brown hands on Rosie's waist and turned her around, directing her back down the stairs. "Her cabin is the one in the stern." Seeing Rosie's uncomprehending look, she added, "The one at the back end of the ship."

"Thank you," Rosie said, trying to quiet the quiver in her stomach. She marched down the passageway, stopping in front of the polished oak door to Octavia's cabin. She reached her hand toward the brass handle and quickly drew it back. She should probably knock first. She hesitated and then rapped twice, so hard she hurt her knuckles.

"Come in," Octavia said.

Rosie opened the door and stood wonderstruck. The stern windows were three rows of square glass panes catching light and reflecting it onto every surface in the cabin. She gathered scattered impressions of a desk with curved legs and inlaid surfaces; a bright carpet patterned with flowers; a shelf of books; another *coton jaune* spread on the bunk, the lace of this one more lavish than that on Tuti's bed; and on the desk, in figured silver frames that spread sunlight in sparkling streaks, two miniatures of Raider—one as he was now, one of him as a boy.

Octavia sat at the desk, her chair turned so that her back was to Rosie, looking out the big bright window at the *Ladyship*'s wake. Her hair hung in a heavy braid down her back, caught at the end with a leather strip. Deflected light burnished the braid's curves, giving her the glow of a halo. She turned to face Rosie, her expression placid, though Rosie thought she could see the shadows of sleeplessness beneath her eyes.

"Did you sleep well?" Octavia asked.

"Too well, I think," Rosie responded. "I was supposed to be put ashore after my burns were treated. That's what Raider—Captain Lyons—said."

"Oh, yes." Octavia leaned forward and rested her elbows on a chart on her desk. "Well, I decided to leave and you were asleep, so ..." She shrugged. "I *am* the captain here. Not Raider."

"But I have to go home," Rosie said. She fought to put steel rather than pleading into her voice. She wanted to be as cool and commanding as the woman before her, the woman who had known Raider for so long that she had a picture of him as a boy.

"I'm so sorry," Octavia said, her face impassive. "I'm afraid that's impossible." She might as well have been talking about the laundry instead of Rosie's whole life.

"But I can't stay on a ship like this," Rosie protested. "It's not—" She stopped abruptly.

"It's not what?" Octavia asked.

Rosie thought she heard amusement under Octavia's calm question, as if she knew Rosie was about to make unflattering remarks about the *Ladyship*'s wholesomeness or safety. She wondered if she was about to be made to walk the plank.

"It's not what?" Octavia repeated.

"It's not ... convenient for you," Rosie replied haltingly. "You said last night you had no place for me."

"Please. Don't concern yourself. Tuti's offered to share her cabin with you, and I'm sure we can find some way for you to occupy yourself while you're with us." Octavia toyed with a brass instrument of some sort on her desk. In a hundred years Rosie couldn't have

51

figured out what to do with it, and Octavia handled it like an old friend.

There didn't seem to be much point in protesting any further. Rosie, being a sensible person, could see she had no leverage. Tuti was right; she'd been wasting her time.

She experienced a queer sense of relief at being forced to accept an inevitability that coincided with a secret and disreputable wish.

Then, remembering her filthy and disheveled condition, she rubbed her hands down the front of her dress. "How long do you think that might be?" she asked. "I don't have anything else to wear."

Octavia's immaculate brow furrowed. "It's always so hard to say how long we'll be at sea. My plan is to put in at The Cove on Tamarind Island for careening. It's overdue, though we did boot-top two months ago." Rosie wouldn't ask for definitions of the unfamiliar words. They didn't matter. "I'd say two weeks to Tamarind. God knows how long before we're back in Campeche." She smiled faintly. "Tuti's clever with a needle. I think she can come up with something for you to wear. Though I'm sure the crew wouldn't mind seeing you in that for the rest of the voyage."

Rosie shook her head. "They might like it, but I wouldn't. I've already been stared at and plagued by enough sailors in the Drop Anchor to last me a lifetime."

Octavia grinned, and suddenly looked much less austere and disconcerting. "Yes, I know that feeling. One must be either very disdainful or very rude, and even that doesn't always discourage such attention. Have you had some breakfast?" At Rosie's negative headshake, she went on. "I'll have Tuti see to that. And . . ." She hesitated momentarily, and Rosie detected the smallest wrinkling of her nose. "And a bath."

Chapter 9

It was a knack she was coming to admire, Rosie thought as she made her way down the passage to Tuti's cabin—the one of establishing control with only cunning words. Both Raider and Octavia did it masterfully. Maybe it was a prerequisite for becoming a ship's captain. If that was the case, Rosie knew she'd never be one. Her talent for stubbornness was one thing; verbal surgery was something much more complicated.

Entering the cabin, she saw Tuti sitting at the table, a tin plate of fruit and biscuits before her. Opposite her was another plate of the same.

Tuti gestured to the plate. "Both the fruit and the biscuits are fresh—a novelty at sea. We have them now only because we were in port yesterday. I hope you will enjoy them. Soon enough it will be back to hardtack and salted beef."

Rosie realized she was ravenous, and the sight of golden biscuits and ripe slices of fruit made her mouth water. She couldn't even pretend indifference; she tucked right in and the food tasted as good as it looked.

"Where did you get that spread?" Tuti asked, pointing to Rosie's embroidered coverlet, folded now at the foot of Tuti's bunk.

"I made it," Rosie said, her mouth full.

"Yes? But it is beautiful. A work of art. Did you embroider, too, those flowers on your dress?"

Rosie looked down at herself and nodded. "There were flowers also around the hem, but they burned off."

"Where did you learn such a thing?"

Such strong memories came from that simple question. Rosie could still remember the look on Father Xavier's face the day she'd appeared at the church of San Francisco, a half mile north of Campeche, her arms full of books, inquiring if he could teach her to read them. She was eight years old and the books had come from a trunk left at the Drop Anchor by a sailor with an overdue rum account. Father Xavier had sorted through the books, selecting those appropriate for a child, and had begun her education.

She couldn't know what a joy it was for him to spend time with the lonely little girl she was, so grateful for his earnest attention, so eager to learn, so receptive. She soothed the sense of failure he felt at his inability to smother the pagan Mayan religion of the Campechans with his gift of Christianity. They came to Mass and still went home to worship their own gods, guardians against storms, and thieves, and snakes.

It was also at the Church of San Francisco that Rosie met Chila, Father Xavier's housekeeper and embroiderer of the beautiful altar cloths. Chila was the one who taught Rosie to sew when, after her lessons with Father Xavier were over, she was reluctant to return to her father and the Drop Anchor. Chila was old and tired and lonely, and sitting in the cool sanctuary or the sun-spattered courtyard with Rosie, guiding the child's small fingers as they learned new stitches, was balm to her spirit.

Father Xavier was ordered to the cathedral in Mérida the week after Chila died of the fever, and the torrents of tears that Rosie wept onto his cassock as she sat helplessly in his lap changed neither event. But the blessings that the two of them had conferred on her, in the form of books, needlework and love, sustained her still.

"An old woman taught me when I was a little girl," Rosie finally answered. "She died, but I kept experimenting and taught myself more. I did work for some of the . . . ladies in Campeche."

She resisted the impulse to tell Tuti more. She knew she was vulnerable to the weakness of being too responsive to anyone who showed a personal interest in her, and she sensed that that would be a mistake aboard this ship. She needed to be as strong and as self-contained as she could be until she was on her own again.

"How did Octavia get to be a ship's captain?" she asked Tuti, turning the conversation away from herself. "I never heard of a woman captain."

"Nor have I," Tuti said. "But Octavia is not like other women."

"Have you known her a long time?"

Tuti poured coffee from a pewter pot into a tin cup for Rosie and pushed it toward her. "Since she was born. I was her nurse."

Rosie couldn't imagine Octavia as a child. Surely she had always been as poised as she was now. Octavia with a skinned knee, throwing a tantrum, whining? Impossible.

"What was she like?" Rosie asked, wiping the juice of a melon slice from her chin with the back of her hand in a way she was sure Octavia never had.

"She was . . . what is the right word?" Tuti answered. "She was *joyeuse*. Gleeful."

"Octavia? Really?" "Gleeful" would have been the last word Rosie would have applied to Octavia.

"Oh, she is different now. Things happen that change

people, you know, *bébé*. Maybe someday she can go back to gleeful. Maybe she is already too far from that to go back.''

Rosie took a sip of coffee from the tin cup and immediately her tongue puckered. "Oooh, something's wrong with the coffee!"

Smile lines meshed with the other lines in Tuti's face and she laughed her raspy laugh. "Nothing is wrong. This is New Orleans coffee, made with chicory. Not everyone likes it at first. But it is good for you. Baptiste says it makes hair on your chest." She laughed her hoarse little laugh again.

Rosie couldn't ever imagine liking it. She felt as if her teeth had been attacked. As for hair on her chest, why, the idea! Remembering the close-up view of Raider's chest she'd had in the Drop Anchor, she wondered if *he* drank New Orleans coffee.

She felt a flush come into her cheeks at the memory, and ducked her head for another bite of biscuit to hide her face from Tuti's wise black eyes. It wouldn't surprise her at all if Tuti knew exactly what was in her mind, and what was there had absolutely no business being there.

Pushing the tin cup away and bending her attention back to Octavia, Rosie asked, "How did she get to be a captain?"

"She wanted to help Raider. Four years ago his brother was impressed by Captain Charles Lawrence. You know of impressment, yes?"

"Isn't it when sailors are taken from one ship to work on another?"

"That puts it very kindly. In reality, it is kidnapping. Because the war with Napoleon has gone on for so long, the British are running out of seamen and they take them where they can find them, mostly from American ships, sometimes from the streets and taverns of ports. For the last four years, Raider has been trying to find his brother and take him back from the British. First alone, then with the help of Octavia, and now, since the war, with the approval of the government.''

"But impressment is legal, isn't it?'' Rosie hadn't paid much attention to the issues of the war between the United States and England. She'd always been too busy and, because she wasn't directly affected, not particularly interested. But she was half English, and Captain Charles Lawrence was the only sailing man in the Drop Anchor who had treated her like a lady; she couldn't help a tendency toward the British point of view.

"Not to Americans,'' Tuti said stiffly.

"But how can Raider hope to know where his brother is after four years?''

"He cannot, of course. But the British say an Englishman cannot change his citizenship, that he is always an Englishman. And they say Americans are still Englishmen, too, in spite of the success of our Revolution. Since seamen are impressed from American ships to become British sailors, it makes sense he could be on an English ship. That is where Raider looks.''

"But surely, after four years . . .''

"Raider will never give up looking,'' Tuti said with a grim set to her mouth. "Never.''

"No wonder Captain Lawrence and Raider seemed so strained with each other that night in the Drop Anchor,'' Rosie said.

"There is more to the story,'' Tuti went on. "In the same battle in which Captain Lawrence took Raider's brother, he left Raider for dead. Raider has more than one reason to hate the man.''

"But why,'' Rosie asked, leaning forward, "should Octavia want to help Raider find his brother?''

Tuti was silent for a moment. Then she looked

straight into Rosie's eyes and said, "Because she loves him."

"Oh," Rosie said. Well, of course, she thought, unsurprised. They made a perfect pair. And before she could stop herself, she asked, "And he?"

"Yes," Tuti said. "As much as he loves his brother. As much as he loves anything."

"Oh," she said again. The biscuit in her mouth didn't taste as good as it had a moment before.

Tuti regarded her for a moment and then stood. "I will bring you some hot water. A bath will make you feel better."

Chapter 10

Tuti was right. Clean skin, clean hair and clean, though borrowed, clothes did help.

Rosie badly wanted to be on deck again, where she could find distraction in the thrilling sight of sun and shadow, sails and sea. This time when she poked her head through the hatch, there were few sailors in sight, and all of them seemed absorbed in their tasks.

As she stepped out onto the deck, wind caught in the bell of the skirt she wore, one of Tuti's with the hem let out to make it long enough, and pulled her toward the bow as if she were a kite. She grabbed onto a capstan to stop herself and found Baptiste sitting at the foot of it, sewing a patch on a pair of pants.

He looked up at her, smiling, and patted the deck next to him. "Sit down before someone runs you up the foremast and makes a staysail of you."

Caught by a vision of herself flying from the foremast, Rosie quickly dropped to his side. The warm wood planking sent heat through the fabric of her skirt. She drew up her knees so she could feel the warmth on the bottoms of her bare feet, and wrapped her arms around her legs, restraining her skirt to modesty.

She found fascinating the contrast between the delicate sewing motions of Baptiste's big tanned hands and the bulky muscles of his bare arms. It hardly seemed that a man shaped as he was would be capable of so domestic an act.

"Something is funny?" he asked.

Rosie hadn't realized until he spoke that she'd been smiling.

"I've never seen a man sew before," she explained.

"A sailor must know how," he said, biting off the thread with his strong white teeth as he finished the patch. "No *mamans,* no wives, no sisters on board to take care of us."

"But there's Octavia and Tuti." She knew it was foolish as soon as she said it. As if anyone, man or woman, could ask Octavia to sew on a button.

Baptiste grinned and the lines of sun and horizons around his eyes deepened. The effect was cheerful and friendly, and when his coffee-brown eyes met Rosie's, they both laughed. It was something Rosie hadn't expected to do again for a long time, and certainly not with someone who looked like Baptiste.

"Octavia cannot tell a needle from a noodle," Baptiste said, unrolling another length of thread and biting it off. "And Tuti might help, but only if it was her idea, not mine. A man is on his own on this ship. On any ship. How are the burns?"

"I can hardly feel them. I don't know what Tuti does, but it works. Some kind of flowers. And cobwebs. She put more on after I bathed. Is she the traitor?" Rosie's father had always said she had more questions than anybody could answer. And he'd certainly had far fewer answers than she had questions.

"Traitor? Oh, you mean *traiteur. Oui,* she is. One of the best. We are lucky to have her with us."

"A *traiteur* isn't the same as a traitor?" Rosie asked, watching as Baptiste's agile fingers mended a three-

60

cornered rip in a shirt. With all her own sewing skill, a three-cornered tear was still the most difficult challenge for her.

"Raider did not explain this to you? No, of course not. One of his tricks, a way to stay in control; never explain anything. *Eh bien,* I have no problems like that, *grâce à Dieu.* A *traiteur* is a Cajun healer. A medicine woman."

Why couldn't Raider have told her at least that much? Rosie wondered, annoyed. Did he get so much pleasure out of scaring people for no good reason?

"Can a man be a *traiteur,* too?" she asked.

"No. Always it is a woman, and always she is descended from another *traiteur.* And always she is left-handed. Do not ask me why," he said, forestalling Rosie, who was about to do just that. "I do not know. That is how it is. Being a *traiteur* is a gift, even a calling, as to a religious life. Some *traiteurs* specialize—in warts, fevers, childbirth or the opposite, causing the miscarriage. Those are called 'angel-makers.' "

Rosie flushed and lowered her eyes.

Baptiste shook his head in amusement. "How old are you?"

"Seventeen," she said. But feeling seven, she thought. "How old are you?"

"Twenty-five. I have almost forgotten what seventeen feels like. But I think my seventeen was different from your seventeen."

She looked at his dark face, his dancing eyes, the gold hoop in his ear. "It wouldn't surprise me a bit," she said. She hesitated over what she wanted to ask next, and then decided to go ahead. Why not? All the rules were new here. "Are you one of the ones who think Raider is losing his mind?" He had said half his crew thought that, and she wanted to know why.

Baptiste laughed, a merry, amused sound. "Raider

told you that, *n'est-ce pas?* More of his battle strategy. If you can keep your opponent afraid of you, you have half the battle won.''

''But I wasn't his opponent. And if he'd left me in Campeche the way I wanted him to, he wouldn't have had to tell me anything.''

''You asked him to leave you?'' Baptiste said, his heavy eyebrows raised. ''And he would not? What did Nic say?''

''Nic wanted him to leave me behind, too. He said, 'The more connections, the more risk.' I don't know what he meant. What *did* he mean?''

Baptiste finished mending the three-cornered tear and held it up to examine. *''Très belle,''* he said, pleased. ''I am getting better at this.'' He put the sewing things away in a small tin box as he spoke. ''He meant the more close people you have in your life, the more people you are involved with, the more people you care about, the more you risk getting hurt if something happens to them. And the more you must think about these close people of yours, the more distracted you become from what you have to do. I do not agree with this. We Cajuns want many attachments. It is better to live a full life, with all its joy and all its pain, than only to exist, *n'est-ce pas?* But Nic, he is different. His wife and children are dead. He takes no more chances.''

''Oh, how terrible.'' She understood that special sort of loss. ''He looks so ferocious, I never even thought of him as somebody who could have a wife and children.''

''I imagine he did not always look so ferocious as he does now. The scar is only four years old. But *peut-être* you can understand why Nic discourages Raider from attachments.''

''I hardly think Raider was attached to me,'' Rosie said. ''He said he was just doing a good deed.''

''Perhaps, *petite*. Perhaps. He does occasionally com-

62

mit a good deed. I think it shall remain one of life's little mysteries. For a time. As for your question—and I have heard this question before—no, I do not think he is mad. Not yet.'' He shrugged his massive shoulders. ''Who can say what will come. And I will know, for I have served with true madmen.'' He grinned, his white teeth flashing. ''I once was a pirate,'' he said with pride. ''In my finest pirate days, I sailed with Jean Laffite.''

Even as isolated as Rosie had been, she knew of Jean Laffite, the daring pirate who preyed on shipping in the Gulf of Mexico and the Caribbean. He had a reputation for boldness and charm and for being almost irresistible to women. Baptiste ceased to seem like the friendly companion she'd begun to think of him and took on a more ominous aspect. With a sigh, she relegated him to her criminal category.

''Do not look so worried, *petite*. I am reformed. A legitimate privateer, that is me. But even Laffite does not think of himself as a pirate. He prefers to be called a corsair. Why torment yourself over names? Look instead into the person.'' He gathered his sewing things and stood. ''If you can.'' His smile was as dazzling as the sunlight glinting off his earring as he strolled away with the graceful, rolling walk of a man long at sea.

Rosie lowered her cheek to her knees and blinked rapidly to keep back tears. She'd just begun to relax under the spell of the sun and the wind and the rhythm of the sea—as well as the companionship of someone willing to answer every question she asked—and now she was feeling the way she had last night, frightened and forlorn.

But what good were tears? What good had they ever done? They hadn't kept Chila alive or prevented Father Xavier from going off to Mérida. They hadn't restored the Drop Anchor or her father or her kitten. What a useless habit crying was.

What was more, she suspected she was being watched by sailors all over the ship and she didn't want to appear as vulnerable as she knew she was. She wanted to be as cool and commanding as Octavia, though she doubted she could ever be haughty enough or rude enough for a whole shipload of men.

Probably *all* of them used to be pirates and were just waiting for the chance to be so again.

In spite of her strongest efforts to the contrary, a fat tear slid down her cheek and soaked into Tuti's skirt.

She felt a touch on her shoulder and heard a voice say, "What's wrong?"

Chapter 11

Hastily wiping her eyes with the hem of her skirt, she looked up into the face of a boy about ten years old. His sharp features were deeply tanned and his shaggy brown hair was streaked with blond from the sun. His brown eyes, as dark as Baptiste's, were narrowed against the sun's glare and alive with curiosity.

"Who are you?" Rosie asked. She felt a lunatic impulse to laugh. Here she was, worried about the unwanted attention of the ship's rough company, all bloodthirsty pirates in her overheated imagination, and the only person to approach her was a little boy.

"Barnaby. I'm the powder boy."

"Powder boy? Do sailors wear powder?"

He laughed so hard he had to sit down, sprawling next to her on the deck. When he could speak, he said, "They don't *wear* it. They use it in their guns. It's my job to keep the ammunition coming during a battle." He sounded quite as competent as the most experienced saltwater man.

"But that's awful!" Rosie cried. "You're just a little boy."

Looking deeply insulted, he drew back his scrawny

shoulders. "I'm a sailor," he said indignantly. "That's my job."

"I don't know what your mother must be thinking, to let you do this. It's far too dangerous for a child."

The look of insult on his little ferret face faded, but his voice kept its edge of toughness. "I ain't got a mother. Not anymore."

Oh, no, Rosie thought. I hope I'm not going to cry again. "I'm sorry," she said. Then she added, "I don't, either."

"You don't?" he asked, interested. "How old were you when she croaked?" He took a coil of rope from his pocket and began tying knots in its length.

"I was three when she cr—when she died. I'm not even sure if I remember her. How old were you?"

"I don't know. Maybe two, maybe three. I don't remember mine, neither, but I'll never forget my pa. I've got the scars to remind me."

"Your father hurt you?" Rosie asked, horrified. Paternal neglect was one thing; abuse, something altogether different.

Barnaby nodded. "He made me stand on the streets in New Orleans and cry and beg for money. When I didn't get as much as he thought I should, he'd—" Barnaby stopped. After a deep breath, he continued. "I did the best I could. Some of the time the bawling was for real but I couldn't *make* people hand over money." He tied another elaborate knot. "I'd rather be a sailor any day."

"But how did you get to be one? Aren't you a little young?" With one finger, Rosie touched the row of knots produced by Barnaby's small, dirty hands.

"It was Captain Lyons. He convinced my pa that I should go to sea with him."

"Yes? How did he do that?"

"First he saw my pa beating me in an alley. Then

66

he gave my pa a lot of money and then he hit my pa so hard he put him to sleep with one punch. Then he took me on the *Avenger*. He said he'd gone to sea at fourteen and he didn't think nine was a bit too soon for me.''

"And how did you get from the *Avenger* to the *Ladyship*?''

"Well, you know, Raider and Octavia are . . .'' He made a sign with his hand that Rosie didn't recognize, but she got the general meaning. "So they meet up every now and then. They own a house on this island, Tamarind Island, and that's mostly where they see each other. They say it's a good place for careening the ships and resting up from battles and things like that, but I think they just like to see each other. Anyway, one time when we was together at The Cove, where their house is, Raider told Octavia how valuable I am''—he made no attempt to sound modest—"and she asked if she could have me on the *Ladyship* for a while and he said all right. He didn't want to, I could tell, but he hates to do anything that might make her sad. It's just that not much happens on the *Ladyship*. There was lots more fighting on the *Avenger*.''

"And you liked all the fighting?'' Rosie asked.

"Sure,'' he said, giving her an incredulous look. "Men arc supposed to fight. But protecting women is important, too, even if it's not as interesting. That's what Raider says, so that's what I do here. I help protect Octavia and Tuti.''

"Octavia looks like she can take care of herself,'' Rosie said, wondering if Raider could have had another motive for getting Barnaby on a safer vessel.

"That's just how she looks. Hey, I've even seen her cry, and I ain't never seen Raider cry. Men don't cry.''

"When did you see Octavia cry?'' Rosie had a hard time imagining such a thing.

67

"When Raider sailed away from The Cove the time he left me with her. She stood on the beach and waved for the longest time, tears dripping right off her chin, and her face never changed at all. I never saw nobody cry like that before. When I cry, my nose runs and my face gets all red and scrunched up." He looked sideways at Rosie. " 'Course, I ain't cried since I was a baby. Fact, I can hardly remember what it's like to cry. I don't even know why I'm talking about it."

"I wish I'd forget how to cry," Rosie said. "My nose runs, too, and besides, crying never does any good. Whatever you're crying about doesn't change."

"Aye," Barnaby said, looking at her. "That's true, ain't it? What was you crying about just now?"

"Oh, something that frightened me. Just something silly. But I'm better now. Can you teach me how to tie knots like these?" Rosie asked, looking at the rope, transformed now into a row of miniature sculptures. "Do they have names?"

He regarded her scornfully. " 'Course they have names. Don't you know anything?" He selected a particularly complicated one. "This here's a wall and crown. Baptiste just taught me that. But the others, I've known how to do them for a long time." Taking up the rope, he showed her other knots, a Flemish knot and a diamond knot and a clove hitch. To Rosie's artisan's eye, the knots had an intricate beauty that she yearned to capture in embroidery.

"If you like these knots, you should see what some of the sailors do with them. Especially Animal. He made a whole hammock out of different kinds of knots."

She didn't even want to ask who Animal was.

"It's what some sailors do to pass the time at sea. Everybody has to do something. Even with all the chores, there's a lot of extra time. And no shortage of rope, either.''

"Can you make things from knots?"

"Naw. I like to tie knots, but not that much. I'm learning other things. Big Tom's teaching me how to play the fiddle, and Max has been showing me how to carve. I like that especially.'' He reached into his pocket and pulled out a perfect little carved puppy dog, one paw up as if to shake hands, his tongue out and a grin on his face.

"Why, Barnaby, he's wonderful!'' Rosie said. "Do you suppose you could make me a kitten? I had a kitten and I've lost him and I miss him. I'd love to have a little wooden one to remind me of my kitty.''

" 'Course I could make you one. His name's Kitty? That's a dumb name for a cat. Especially a boy cat. He needs a better name than that.''

"Well, the truth is, I never got around to giving him a proper name. I didn't have him long enough. I just hope he isn't being called soup by now.''

"Soup?''

"He's on the *Avenger*. Nicodemus McNair threatened to make soup of him.''

Barnaby sat up straighter. "He might do it, too. Ain't he something to look at? If a person wasn't brave, he might give you nightmares. How come he has your kitten?''

Rosie told him a little of how she came to be on the *Ladyship*, not mentioning that Raider had killed her father.

"Well, just in case your cat's still alive,'' Barnaby said, meaning to cheer her up, but not succeeding, "let's think of a good name for him. Not Kitty! What about Killer? Or Jolly Roger? How about Warrior?''

"I don't think—''

"I know! How about Midshipman? That'd make him a real sailor."

"Midshipman? That name's bigger than he is. But Middy, that sounds good." Sort of like Kitty, she thought, but didn't say so. "A good name for a seafaring cat." Rosie hoped Middy was still seafaring and not traveling in someone's stomach.

Some bells clanged and Barnaby stood up. "I've got to go help Tiny in the galley. It's one of my jobs." He looked a little embarrassed. "On a ship, sometimes the men have to do women's jobs."

Rosie smiled up at him. "I've always admired a man who can do a lot of things. It means he's more talented than most."

"Really?" Barnaby said. "Well, I've always thought that, too. It's good you agree with me."

After Barnaby left, Rosie sat for a while longer on the deck, uneasily aware of the looks she got from the passing sailors, though none of them spoke to her. Finally she couldn't stand any more of it, and though she regretted leaving the sunny spot by the foremast, she went belowdecks to Tuti's cabin.

Tuti sat at the table writing in a large green leather-bound book. When Rosie entered, Tuti scattered sand over what she had written and waited for it to dry.

"I'm sorry," Rosie said. "I didn't mean to interrupt you. I can leave." She began to back out the door.

"No, no," Tuti said. "I am finished. I keep records in this book of the treatments I give. I was writing about your burns." She smiled. "Not a very interesting wound, *bébé,* but I do not think you would like having an interesting one." She tapped the sand from her pages into an ornate silver sandbox.

Rosie sat in the other chair. "I don't think so, either." She pulled her skirt aside and looked at the pads

70

of cobwebs stuck to her burns. "They feel nearly healed already."

"They were not so very bad to begin with," Tuti said. "Raider worried for no reason."

"I told him that. But I got the impression he likes to be the one to make the decisions."

Tuti laughed her little cackle. "You are correct; he is arrogant." She looked seriously at Rosie. "But do not forget, he is also decent." She took her clay pipe from the pocket in her skirt, filled it with tobacco and lit it. Fragrant coils of smoke rose to the low ceiling of the cabin.

Rosie didn't want to talk about Raider. She didn't want to think about him, or about Middy, or about her father or Barnaby or Baptiste or anything. She wanted to close her eyes and wake up in Campeche and find that everything that had happened in the past two days was a dream. Raider and Octavia and all the rest of them could remain the stuff of her escape fantasies—fantasies in which Rosie was the one who got to make the decisions and direct the action.

"You seem tired," Tuti said.

"Too much sun," Rosie said. "Too much everything."

Chapter 12

Rosie had been alone in Tuti's cabin with nothing to do for a long time. She didn't know where Tuti had gone or when she was coming back.

Idleness was something new for Rosie; always before, she'd felt the press of duties to be done, but now there was nothing clamoring for her attention. She couldn't even read Tuti's books, because they were all in French. Much as she'd always thought she'd enjoy being a lady of leisure, she found it made her fidgety. If only she had a needle and thread, she'd know what to do with herself.

She stood for a long while with her forearms on the sill of the open window, watching the crests of white water rush by the *Ladyship*'s hull. Every peaked wave took her farther from Campeche and closer to ... to what?

When Barnaby banged through the door with a tray in his hands, she jumped up from the bunk, where she'd been examining the handmade lace on the *coton jaune* spread.

"Hello," she cried.

He gave her a startled look and said, "I brought you some dinner. I had to make the soup."

He sounded so ill-treated, Rosie almost laughed. "A man who can make soup *and* fight on a privateer is quite rare and remarkable," she said, coming over to the table. "I'll wager Captain Lyons can't make soup. Even out of my ki—Middy."

Barnaby frowned and shrugged. "I put in lots of cabbage, so you won't get scurvy."

"What's scurvy?" she asked. "Never mind. Not before dinner. Can you come eat with me? I hate eating alone."

"Well . . ." He pondered the request. "Usually I eat with the other men in the forecastle, but I guess they'd understand if I told them you needed me. I'll go get my plate." He went off with dignity, squaring his thin shoulders.

Tuti returned just as they were finishing their meal, bringing her own cup of coffee with her. Rosie wondered where she had eaten, and with whom.

After Barnaby had taken the dishes and gone back to the galley, Tuti said to Rosie, "Come over here. By the window."

"Why?" Rosie asked.

"I want to look at you. Come here."

"But you've already looked at me," Rosie said, coming to the window anyway.

Tuti took Rosie's chin in her hand and turned her face from side to side in the strong, slanting light from the window. "Good skin," she said. "What do you do for it?"

What were the things that other women did for their skin that she knew nothing about? Again, as she so often did, she felt the lack of knowledge she was sure a mother would have given her. "I wash it, that's all," she said apologetically.

"I know a hundred women who would hate you for that," Tuti said.

"For washing my face?" Rosie asked, astounded.

Tuti's laugh rasped. "For having *only* to wash it. Look at this texture. Like a flower petal. What did your mother look like?"

Rosie almost said she could show Tuti a picture of her mother before she remembered that Raider had taken her locket. "She was very beautiful. I wish I looked like her. I'm small, like she was, but she was delicate and I'm sturdy. And my chin's too square and my mouth's uneven. My father always told me I'd never be as pretty as she was. He called her the Countess, when he was still talking about her. And her hair! So thick and dark and styled like she really was a countess."

Tuti's small hand moved from Rosie's chin to her hair. She picked up a strand and let it run through her fingers. "Your father was a fool. And you do have your mother's hair. Thick and heavy, like satin."

Tuti thought her father was a fool? He was, of course, but how could Tuti know? "Oh, no. Mine's too heavy and too curly. It's always in a tangle and it can't be styled. I've tried."

"When was it last cut?" Tuti asked.

"I don't remember. A long time ago. Why?"

"It needs cutting again. Not a great amount, but very cleverly. I can do that. And you tell me all that color in your cheeks is natural?"

"Tuti, you saw me when I came on board. I didn't have a thing with me. I used to watch La Señora's ladies paint their faces, and once I tried it. But they laughed at me when I was finished."

"Huh," Tuti snorted. "They know nothing. And are selfish and jealous as well. I am a better teacher for you."

"Teacher?" Rosie asked. "For what? What does it matter what my skin looks like? Or my hair?"

"With the smallest effort, I can make you a beauty," Tuti said. "May I?"

In her most elaborate fantasies, this was never what Rosie could have imagined would happen to her on this ship. "I don't believe you," she said. "And even if you could do that, why would you want to?"

Tuti smiled. "So you can begin to think of yourself as someone else. Your old life is gone, don't you know that? Something new begins now. You must be ready."

"But what? What's beginning now?"

"Ah, you will see. In time."

Rosie felt the way she had the morning before, when she had stood on the deck of the *Ladyship* for the first time in daylight: exhilarated and shivery with anticipation.

"All right," she told Tuti. "Make me ready for what's to come."

Two hours later, Tuti at last let Rosie look into a mirror. When she did, she wasn't sure she was looking at herself. Tuti had cut her hair so that it fell neatly just below her shoulders instead of raggedly to the middle of her back. Then she'd washed it with a sweet-smelling soap that Tuti said she made herself, and rinsed it in weak chamomile tea. Rosie had resisted the tea, but Tuti promised her it would remove all the soap residue and leave her hair shining. To Rosie's surprise, that was exactly what it had done. Then Tuti had trimmed the hair around Rosie's face so that it lay in feathery wisps that curved into curls as it dried.

"Is this really my own hair?" Rosie asked, turning her head before the mirror.

Tuti gave a satisfied chuckle and tugged at the strands around Rosie's face, arranging them just right. "Your own face, too," she said, "but in a new frame. It makes a difference, *non*?"

The haircutting wasn't the only magic Tuti performed. She washed Rosie's face with some concoction that turned the water green, and scrubbed her with so rough a cloth Rosie half expected to look like raw meat. Instead, in the mirror her skin looked clear and glowing, and somehow her eyes looked bigger and darker blue.

The final surprise came when Tuti pierced her ears. Rosie wasn't expecting the first pierce, thinking that the way Tuti pinched her earlobe was part of this mysterious project of creating beauty. Pinching numbed the ear some, but not enough, and the pain was such that she yelped and then, furiously, told Tuti she didn't want the other one done. Why should she have pierced ears when she didn't own any earrings?

"Octavia has a chest full of earrings, and of other jewels, too," Tuti soothed her. "Things from some of the ships we have taken. She means to sell most of them when we return to New Orleans, but for now, you may have your choice."

She went off to Octavia's cabin and returned with a large carved box brimming with jewels.

"Are those real?" Rosie asked, wide-eyed. "But they're, they're ..." She couldn't think of an appropriate word.

"Beautiful?" Tuti asked. "*Oui.* Except perhaps for this." She dangled a heavy bracelet, crusted with huge rubies, clusters of diamonds and an elaborate clasp, from her forefinger. "A bit *de trop,* I think."

"No," Rosie said. "I mean, yes, they're beautiful, but it's so *much.* Too much. How could one person wear all that?"

"Well, not all at the same time, *bébé,*" Tuti said, smiling indulgently. "Besides, they didn't all belong to the same person." She stirred around in the box until she found a pair of sapphire studs rimmed with tiny diamonds. "These," she said decisively. "To match your eyes."

Rosie went from never wanting her other ear pierced to hardly being able to wait to see how the sapphire earrings would look in her ears.

"Now," Tuti said, "while I take care of this other ear, I think you must tell me your story, and how you came to arrive here in Raider's gig."

As Tuti pierced Rosie's remaining ear and threaded both holes with black silk thread until they healed enough for the sapphire earrings, Rosie, contrary to her promise to herself but unable to resist Tuti's interest, spoke about her life in Campeche and the scraps of what she remembered of life before that.

A sunset light had settled into the cabin, and the gathering shades of dusk lent an air of hushed intimacy to the fragrant space. The shipboard sounds that Rosie had already become accustomed to wove softly behind her words as she told Tuti about her past.

Chapter 13

"*Eh bien,* this explains much," Tuti said, brushing Rosie's hair with an ivory-backed brush. "How you know so much of some things and so little of others."

"The things I know about don't seem to be the ones I need," Rosie said, feeling slightly hypnotized by the soothing brush strokes and the fading light. "There's so much I don't understand that everyone else seems to take for granted. Barnaby's probably smarter than me about some things."

"Probably," Tuti said. "But not all things are important to know. And the important things, well, life will teach you those if you care to learn. And some of them you know already. Yes, you do," Tuti added when Rosie turned and gave her a skeptical look.

Tuti put down the hairbrush and lit the lantern. She took a folded hammock from one of her cupboards and hung it from hooks already in the wall. "You've slept in a hammock before, yes?" she asked Rosie.

"Well, no. My father insisted on real beds, even though most everybody in Campeche sleeps in hammocks. He said he wasn't going to learn to sleep in one because he didn't intend to stay. I always wanted one—

nothing could have been more uncomfortable than those awful straw mattresses we did sleep on, and the hammocks were so pretty. The grandmothers would sit in front of their houses making them, and sometimes they'd put in colored yarn and fancy fringe at the ends. I thought sleeping in a hammock would be like being in a cradle.''

''*Oui,* so it is, and more, at sea.'' She showed Rosie how to get in and out of the hammock without being tossed to the floor, then said, ''I must speak with Octavia for a time. I will have someone bring you something to eat. Go to sleep when you wish, and I will be silent when I return.''

''All right. And, Tuti,'' she said, ''thank you for . . .'' She gestured to herself.

''It was a pleasure for me also,'' Tuti said and laid her small brown hand on Rosie's cheek. *''Bonsoir, bébé.''*

Soon after Tuti left, Rosie's supper was brought to her by an enormously tall man with a very deep voice who introduced himself as Big Tom and said he was the sailing master. It seemed to Rosie that he took up all the room and most of the air in the cabin, and she waited for him to leave so she could eat.

He leaned against the wall by the door and crossed his arms over his chest. ''Thank you for bringing my supper,'' she said, still standing behind her chair at the table.

He waved his big hand. ''There wasn't a way to choose from all the ones who wanted to without causing a riot. Only thing for it was to bring it myself.''

''Well, thank you,'' she said again.

''Best eat it while it's hot,'' he said, giving no indication of leaving.

So Rosie sat down and tried to eat with Big Tom watching her every move.

After a few minutes of difficult swallowing under his stolid scrutiny, she couldn't contain herself. She put her fork down on the tin plate and said, "You know, it's very hard for me to eat with you watching me as if I were *your* next meal. Do you have to do that?"

"Beg pardon," Big Tom replied. "You're a curiosity aboard, is what it is. We're curious, we are. We don't even know your name. What is it?"

As long as Tuti thought her old life was over, she might as well get rid of that whole big mouthful that had been her name. Everybody who ever heard it made fun of it, even though she'd always loved it for its elegant sound. She was sure the name had been her mother's idea, a way to combine both her English and her Portuguese heritages in one package.

If she'd known she was going to have to come up with a new name for her new situation, she could have spent some time thinking of something interesting, but for now— "Rosie," she said. "Just Rosie."

"Most sailors think a woman aboard's bad luck," he said, "but we ain't like them, since we've got a woman captain. We're what you could call tolerant. Of some things. Of the things we decide to be tolerant of. Everything else we hate. But if Raider wants you aboard, then it's all right with us. Besides, I told the boys that if any one of them gives you a bit of trouble, I'll have him . . . never mind. I forgot you was eating."

She choked on the bite she'd just taken. "Well, thank you, that's very . . ." She trailed off.

"Not to be saying anything about how you look, either," Big Tom went on, settling himself more comfortably against the wall, "because we all agree you're a fine-looking female, but you ain't the kind that usually interests Raider. He likes them either painted up like a

80

porcelain doll or cool, like Captain Octavia. I never seen him go for something like you."

What did *that* mean, Rosie wondered, "something like you"? And how could Octavia tolerate knowing he was with other women? Or was their relationship such an extraordinary one, between two such extraordinary people, that she felt no threat from those other, painted women?

As for his interest in *her*—Rosie took a deep breath and looked straight at Big Tom. "I can assure you that your friend Raider has absolutely no interest in me. I'm just some ... some accident that happened to him. I have no idea why you've assumed something more than that." Then she added, knowing it wasn't strictly the truth anymore, "I'd go home to Campeche right now if I could get Octavia to turn this boat around."

Sounding very nearly shocked, Big Tom said, "Don't ever call the *Ladyship* a boat. Or the *Avenger,* either. They're ships. And they're *shes.*"

"Well, I'm sorry," Rosie said stoutly, "about the ship part. But everything else I said is the truth."

"Uh-huh. Still and all, that was quite a good-bye Raider gave you last night." Big Tom sounded as if he were smiling, but Rosie wouldn't look at him to be sure.

"I can't explain that," she said, her eyes on her supper. "It just ... happened."

"Uh-huh," he said again. "From what I've seen, very little 'just happens' to Raider."

"Well, lately a lot has been 'just happening' to me." Rosie pushed her plate across the table toward him. "I don't want any more."

Big Tom picked up the plate. "Pleasant dreams, then," he said, still sounding as if he were smiling. He left, closing the door behind him.

After Big Tom left, Rosie took off her borrowed skirt

81

and shirt and, wearing only her borrowed chemise, wrapped herself in a soft blanket. She felt naked in more ways than one as she looked out over the moon-silvered water.

What lessons was life trying to teach her now? she wondered.

She touched the silk loops in her sore earlobes, and the wisps of hair on her forehead, and went to bed in her borrowed hammock. As she nestled into Tuti's blanket, she wondered if it, too, was part of her *L'Amour de Maman*.

What she had suspected was true; sleeping in a hammock was like being rocked all night long. The gentle creaking sounds of the ship's ropes and timbers, the soft voices as sailors on watch called to each other, the pungent aroma of tobacco smoke, all twined through Rosie's dreams, creating a peaceful snugness that her starved soul craved. She was held in drifting calm through the dark hours, and the small sounds Tuti made when at last she came to bed served only to increase Rosie's floating impression that everything was being cared for by people who knew what they were doing.

The irony of feeling safer here at sea in the midst of a war than she ever had in Campeche with her feckless father was not lost on her, even in her sleep.

Chapter 14

The next morning Rosie woke to find Tuti already gone and a plate of breakfast waiting on the table. She felt not a moment's disorientation, only a surprising surge of gratitude that she had not dreamed the *Ladyship*.

She washed, dressed and ate, then climbed the steps to the deck again. Standing beside the hatchway, she experienced a soaring joy at the sight of the billowed sails, the hard blue sky and the strong, busy sailors.

"I hope your stay with us is not proving too tedious," Octavia said beside her.

Rosie jumped. "Oh, I didn't hear you!"

"Forgive me." Then, looking more closely at her, Octavia said, "Tuti told me she'd tended to your needs, but I can see she's done more than that."

Rosie touched her hair self-consciously. "She told me I needed to be ready for new things. This is supposed to help."

Octavia smiled slightly. "Tuti is usually right. And she isn't happy without someone to fuss over. An excellent attribute in a *traiteur*, I suppose. I must say she's made quite a difference in you."

"Thank you." I think, Rosie thought. She looked

down at her hands, wishing Octavia's grace didn't make her feel so simple and clumsy.

"Would you like to see the rest of the *Ladyship*?" Octavia asked.

"Oh, very much. I think it's—I mean *she's* the most beautiful bo—ship I've ever seen."

Octavia smiled again, fully this time and with genuine pleasure. The act warmed the beauty of her flawless face. "She *is* a beautiful ship. I'm fortunate. She was a gift from my father, designed to my specifications."

Rosie couldn't think of a more perfect present for someone like Octavia. Jewels would be wasted on her; she would outshine them.

"You must have a very generous father," Rosie said, trying to remember if Percy had ever given her any kind of a gift at all. Nothing came to her mind.

"Yes, he is. But although he gave me the ship, he's not happy about me sailing around out here."

"Well, it is dangerous," Rosie said. "But what else did he think you were going to do with the *Ladyship*?"

"He knew. And he also knew better than to try to stop me," Octavia said. "He wanted to come with me."

"He did?"

"Partly to look out for me, but mostly to be in on the fun."

"Fun?" Rosie said. But even as she uttered the word, she realized she understood what Octavia meant. Not that the fighting part was fun, but the being-at-sea part, with the sun and sky and wind and full, towering sails; that part had already been fun for her.

"It has its moments," Octavia replied, "if you're a lover of excitement and risk as my father is. He didn't think a convent education prepared me for this."

"I can't think that *would* prepare you," Rosie said, wondering if that convent education was what accounted for Octavia's perfect poise. At least *she'd* had

Father Xavier and Chila for a year and a half. It was some help.

"That's exactly what I told my father," Octavia said, a touch of warmth in her voice.

Rosie felt absurdly pleased.

"I told him to stay home and tend to his business, that the *Ladyship* was my business. Shall we have a look?" And she went off without waiting for an answer, her white skirt and shirt catching the wind and the sun. Rosie followed, thinking how much she envied Octavia's unusual position in the world; a woman who could do what she wanted with her life, and be damned to anyone who wanted her to do otherwise.

By the time Rosie had followed Octavia around for an hour, her head was a jumble of new sights and new words.

She'd been shown how to load a cannon, how to holystone the deck, how the cordwainer sewed together a leather powder bucket, where the barrels of apples and flour, potatoes and dried fish were stored, as well as the supplies of pikes, muskets, cutlasses and boarding nets.

She'd observed, with a barely controlled fascination, the sailors in the forecastle washing their clothes, playing cards, studying navigation from Bowditch's *Practical Navigator*—and they had observed her in return, not bothering in the least to control their own curiosity.

And the sails! She'd had no idea there were so many kinds. She knew she'd never be able to keep them all straight: studding sails and water sails, ringtails and moonrakers, mizzen topgallants and spankers.

There was much more to being a sailor, she was learning, than coming aboard and pulling up the anchor.

The tour ended in Octavia's handsome cabin. Octavia moved around, her slender fingers lightly touching her possessions, as if she were reassuring herself they were still there, before she sat in the chair behind the desk. "Sit down, Miss Fielding," she said, gesturing to the other chair. "Well, what do you think?"

Rosie sat. "You can call me Rosie," she said, and went on. "It's—I mean *she's* absolutely beautiful. And complicated. I don't know how you keep everything so organized."

"Organization's the most important thing on board a ship. You must know where everything is at every moment. An emergency could arise at any time—a fire, a storm, an attack—and there would be no time to hunt for what you needed."

"Of course," Rosie said. "That's very sensible." Then she blurted the question that had been on her mind since she'd first seen Octavia. "Do you really like living like this?"

Octavia didn't seem offended by Rosie's curiosity. She turned to look out the bright stern windows. "Yes," she said slowly. "Sometimes. I like the freedom. The simplicity. The changing beauty of the sea. I hate the reason I'm here."

"But if you hate it, why do you—" As long as she was getting answers, it was almost impossible for Rosie to stop asking questions.

Before she could finish, Octavia said, "I have no choice."

From the tone of Octavia's voice, Rosie knew she'd asked enough questions. She wouldn't have known what to say next anyhow. Octavia must love Raider very much to feel she had no choice but to help him find his brother.

Octavia turned back to face her. "As long as you'll be with us for a while, did you see anything that especially interested you? Perhaps we can put you to work, to help you pass the time."

Rosie thought of all the jobs she wouldn't want. She wouldn't want to holystone the deck, or pick oakum, or splice ropes. She wouldn't want to clean cannons or work in the stuffy, odiferous galley. All she wanted to do was feel the wind and the sun on her body, to watch the constantly changing face of the water, to experience the living motion of the ship.

"Do you think I could learn to climb in the rigging?" she asked. "Maybe I could be a lookout."

Octavia laughed, the first time Rosie had heard her do so. It was a short laugh, with no trace of childlike glee. "That's one thing I'm afraid to do," she said. "But Baptiste could teach you. He loves it." She regarded Rosie evenly. "So does Raider."

It didn't surprise Rosie that Raider and Baptiste would like it, but she couldn't believe Octavia was afraid of anything.

And if Octavia was afraid of being in the rigging, what in the world was Rosie thinking of?

Chapter 15

Tuti found Rosie a pair of breeches to put on and, when she protested, painted a vivid picture of what could happen to her aloft in a skirt. Rosie donned the pants without further protest, except to ask whose they were.

"I will not say," Tuti told her, "except that nearly every man on board said he would be happy to take his pants off for you." She laughed hoarsely.

"Well, it's not mutual," Rosie said, holding the too-large waistband against her as Tuti belted the pants with a scarf. "I'm not interested in any man, ever."

"So you say now," Tuti said, knotting the scarf.

"So I'll always say. I'm going to live with all the orphaned children I can afford to take care of, and a lot of animals. No matter how many of them there are, they won't be as much trouble as one man."

"We can talk about this later," Tuti replied. "For now, Baptiste is waiting for you."

"There's nothing more to talk about."

"Perhaps I know more about this than you do. But later, *bébé*."

Then Tuti bound up Rosie's hair in a head scarf, which she called a *tignon*. "One moment with hair in your eyes could mean your death," Tuti said. "Now go along. Learn something new."

Rosie stood on the deck with Baptiste, watching Barnaby give a showy demonstration of running through the rigging. She wasn't sure now that this was such a good idea. Barnaby was so far above her, she could hardly tell what he was doing, much less imagine herself doing the same thing.

But, oh, if she could learn, then she could be inside the wind and the sky.

"First thing," Baptiste said to her. "Always go up on the weather side."

"I don't even know what that means," Rosie said. "Maybe I should learn how to holystone the deck instead."

"No, no, *petite*. You have done enough of that sort of thing. You will see. It is a thrill like no other. The weather side is the side the wind comes from. Watch the sails and you can tell. If you go up the weather side, the wind will blow you into the ropes, not off them. You see? *Très logique*. Perfectly sensible. Now, up you go."

Baptiste's strong hands fastened around her waist, almost meeting each other, and lifted her up so high her bare feet encountered rope footholds nearly at the level of his waist. In an instant he was beside her, one arm looped around a backstay as his other arm steadied her.

"Do not look down," he said sternly. "Go up one foot at a time, as if you are climbing a ladder."

"I've climbed a ladder before," Rosie said faintly. "But never one as tall as this. And never one that was moving at high speed."

Baptiste laughed so loud that several sailors on the deck turned to look up at him.

"So now you will have that experience," he said. "One foot up." He climbed above her and Rosie, afraid of being left behind, climbed staunchly up, holding onto the shrouds so tightly her hands ached, until she was beside him again. "You see," he said, smiling his buoyant smile. "Easy."

"Come on, Rosie," Barnaby called from far above her. "Come on. What's wrong? Are you scared?"

If a little boy could get that far up, surely she could. Rosie took another step up. Warm wind whipped at her shirt and tugged at her *tignon*. She could feel the way it pressed her into the ropes, and she relaxed a little. She felt almost that the wind would hold her there even if she let go with her hands.

With Baptiste's patient encouragement—"One step more. Now another. That is right. Very fine. Now one step more"—she finally reached Barnaby, hanging nonchalantly on the main-topgallant yard.

The sway of the ship was exaggerated this high up, and Rosie seemed to swing from one compass point to another in a way that made her head reel. She looked down into the foaming water as the *Ladyship,* which seemed impossibly small from such a height, sliced through the sea, and could see herself pitched down into it, tumbling from her precarious perch.

In her vivid imagination, she could feel the cold turmoil of the water as she struck it, could see the green depths pulling her down, down, her hair drifting upward past her face as she sank. How far was it to the bottom, and what creatures would she pass on the way? What would happen when she had at last to take a breath, and could inhale only water? She had never associated the warm, friendly tide of her Campechan beaches with such impersonal, killing force, and yet it was the same sea.

Her heart rattled against the cage of her ribs and her

breath came in quick gasps. Then she felt Baptiste's calm hand on her shoulder.

"Keep your eyes on the horizon," he told her. "That way you do not feel the roll so much. Well? What do you think? Magnificent, is it not?"

"Magnificent" was not the first word that occurred to Rosie. But, bracketed by her beaming companions, with Baptiste's hand still on her shoulder, she was able to bring her sprinting heart under control.

"It definitely is," she said. "I'm sure there's nothing to match it. But I believe I'll think it's even more magnificent once I'm back on deck." She twined her hands more tightly into the ratlines.

"It is good to respect the ship and the sea, yes," Baptiste said. "This will keep you careful. But once you are careful . . . ah, *petite,* look out there. See how beautiful—the sky, the sea, our fine ship."

Baptiste was right. It was beautiful up here. Almost as if she were flying, a part of the wind and the sky.

Still, she couldn't help wondering if birds ever looked down and got dizzy when they realized how high up they were.

"There is only one thing more a man needs to be happy," Baptiste said.

"What?" asked Rosie.

He looked at her, his dark eyes merry. "My seventeen was surely different from your seventeen."

"Oh, that," Rosie said. "You mean a woman. Any woman." She snorted. "Men!"

"No, no, *petite*. Not just any woman. What a man needs to be happy is—"

"A sail!" Barnaby cried.

Rosie actually would have liked to hear what would make Baptiste happy. Undoubtedly it would be interesting, though probably not something suitable for discussion in polite company, which most certainly Rosie wasn't in.

"Look!" Barnaby pointed to the horizon, and Rosie, following his finger, could see the mast peaks of a ship. She felt like a ninny for hoping it was the *Avenger.*

"Go, Barnaby," Baptiste ordered. "Tell Octavia."

Barnaby scampered down through the rigging faster than a monkey and hit the deck while Rosie was still trying to determine how to place her feet for her first step down.

With Baptiste's encouragement, Rosie descended. By the time they gained the deck, it was swarming with sailors preparing the *Ladyship* to make chase. Men raced past Rosie, taking the place she had just vacated, to unfurl more sail.

Baptiste's face was alive with excitement, his white teeth and dark eyes shining. "Watch, *petite,* as we hang out the wash. No ship can escape us!"

"Hang out the wash?" Rosie echoed. "I thought we were going after that ship."

His big laugh carried to the top of the mainmast. "We are! Hanging out the wash means packing on sail. I must go. And you must stay out of the way. Over there, by the capstan where we talked yesterday. Sit and watch."

Rosie did as she was told, even though she seemed to be the only one aboard with nothing to do. Barnaby ran, piling muskets and pikes in strategic locations along the deck. Tuti helped to string the boarding nets, Big Tom's booming voice relayed Octavia's orders for changes in the set of the sails and Octavia herself was everywhere, supervising everything. Rosie had never felt more useless.

The *Ladyship* flew before the wind, sails close-hauled and taut, and spray leapt over the bow as she breasted the waves. Rosie braced herself against the capstan and watched for the sails of the other ship. She knew it wasn't the *Avenger*; they wouldn't be arming the cannon if it was Raider's ship.

Barnaby stopped beside her, a load of muskets in his arms. "Oh, ain't it fine!" he cried. "See how fast she goes! She can steal the wind right out of the sky."

"But the other ship seems to be going just as fast," Rosie said. "I can't see that we're getting any closer."

"We will, we will," he assured her. "Nobody can outrun the *Ladyship*."

But as the time passed, it seemed that the other ship was doing exactly that. She stayed within sight, but the distance between them remained the same. With dusk came clouds streaming past the horizon and covering the darkening sky.

Rosie was stiff from sitting so long and from the unreleased tension in her muscles. Barnaby came again and sat beside her as a sailor went around them to light the deck lanterns. An atmosphere of strained expectation filled the ship and infected Rosie, too, even though she didn't know what would happen when they overtook the other ship.

"Why haven't we caught her yet?" Rosie asked Barnaby.

"She's got a whizzer of a captain," he said. "He's finding the same wind we are, and his ship must be as trim. We won't catch her in the dark. Oh, I hope they don't get away in the night. If we can keep up, we'll take them in the morning."

"You mean we have to wait? But everyone's so ready."

"Aye, we're ready, but we can't board a ship a league away even if we could see her in the dark. We might as well have something to eat and settle for the night so we can be fresh for the fight in the morning."

Chapter 16

Rosie slept poorly that night, disturbed by her own imagination as well as by the sounds of a shipful of seamen too restless for sleep. Just before dawn, Tuti rose and dressed, and when Rosie moved to get up, too, Tuti pressed her back into the hammock.

"Sleep while you can, *bébé*," she said. "You can do nothing now but stay out of the way and be safe. You will know when is the time to get up." She patted Rosie's cheek and left the cabin, and Rosie went back to sleep feeling like a cosseted child.

She was awakened by the sound of cannon fire. The *Ladyship* lurched and shuddered, but Rosie couldn't tell if that was the result of firing her own cannon or of being struck by someone else's.

She jumped out of the hammock, her heart hammering and her throat dry, staggered against the table as the *Ladyship* heeled, and ran to the window.

She saw nothing but frolicking blue ocean and a wide sky empty of clouds. How could such ordinary beauty exist on this side of the ship, while on the other ... She had to find out what was on the other side.

Quickly she dressed, deciding on the breeches again

instead of a skirt. She could move faster in pants and was afraid she might have to.

The acrid smell of powder filled the passage as she hurried to the hatchway. She could hear running footsteps and shouts and the clang of steel on steel. At the top of the hatch she caught a moment's glimpse of a forest of sail, the crowded masts of the other ship, before the impact of the two hulls colliding threw her to the foot of the steps. Bruised, yet more curious than frightened, she got to her hands and knees and crept up the steps again.

With only her nose peeking above the level of the deck, Rosie could see Baptiste throwing a grappling hook across to the other ship. A boiling mass of seamen lined the gunwales of both ships. Most of them were stripped to the waist and sweating; all of them were bristling with weapons. Their cutlasses caught the morning sun and threw its refractions in scattered arcs across the crowded decks.

As Rosie watched, men from the *Ladyship* flung themselves over the side and onto the deck of the other ship, to hack and slice at that crew with their fiery blades.

At the first spurt of blood, Rosie hid her face in her hands, assaulted by reality. The shouting and the screams of the wounded hurt her ears and she knew that those sounds would stay in her memory forever.

Where was Tuti? And Octavia? And Barnaby! Tough little Barnaby, who so loved a fight, would be in the thick of it, where he could get . . . Rosie removed her hands from her face and forced herself to look out through the hatch again.

Men from the other ship had managed to board the *Ladyship* now, though she couldn't tell how many. She didn't know the faces of the *Ladyship*'s crew well enough to tell them apart.

She saw Baptiste, his face a savage mask, raise his cutlass over his head and begin to bring it down on a man with a knife in each hand. Rosie buried her face again, and when she was once more able to look, Baptiste was nowhere in sight.

She raised her eyes to the rigging, remembering the fear and exhilaration she had felt there yesterday, but feeling only fear now. Up there, far above the fighting, she saw Barnaby standing on a spar, his arm around the mizzenmast for support, watching the deck below. She thanked everything she could think of that he was smart enough to remove himself to a safe place.

And then she saw a man climbing carefully in the rigging, behind Barnaby and out of his sight, a dagger in his teeth.

Rosie shouted to Barnaby, but the noise was so great from the clash of weapons, the musket fire, the cries from men's throats, she knew he wouldn't hear her. She looked for Baptiste, or Tuti, or any familiar face, to send that person to help Barnaby, but she saw no one.

She couldn't go out on the deck, she knew she couldn't. There was too much blood, too much noise, too much danger. But Barnaby—she looked and saw the man edging closer to him. Even if she *could* go out there, what would she do then? She was unarmed and far from sure-footed in the rigging.

She looked up at the man and Barnaby again and crept out through the hatch.

Crouching by a stanchion, she looked for a path through the fighting. The noise was louder here, and the smell—she didn't know what it was, a combination of blood and fear and sweat—almost made her sick. As she gathered her courage for a sprint to the mizzen, a man's body fell to the deck next to her, his blood spattering onto her shirt. His eyes met hers as he lay in his own blood, and she thought there was surprise in them—at seeing her or at what had happened to him, she couldn't tell. While she watched, they glazed over and the light in them dimmed.

She sprang up, ran for the foot of the mizzenmast, hoisted herself up into the shrouds, remembering to stay on the weather side, and climbed as fast as she could. The man was above her but still below Barnaby, though slowly, carefully, getting nearer.

She had no idea what she would do when she got to him. But by that time she would be close enough to call to Barnaby and for him to hear her. Then he could get away.

Then, she hoped, she, too, could get away.

If only Barnaby would look around instead of fastening his gaze so intently on the fighting on the deck below him.

She watched the ratlines under her hands, she watched the horizon, she watched the strange man above her, but she didn't look down at the blood-slicked deck. And she went up fast. Now she could almost touch the man above her and she could certainly call to Barnaby.

"Barnaby!" she shouted. "Go down!"

He turned, and so did the man above her. His mouth opened in surprise before he remembered he held a dagger in his teeth. It dropped, but with one sure movement he caught it by the handle as it fell past his waist.

"What's this?" he asked. "A girl in the rigging? Don't ye know ye've spoiled my fun? Ye'll have to pay for that, ye know." He swiped at her with the dagger, though she was too far below for him to reach her. It frightened her nevertheless and she started so violently that she almost threw herself out of the ropes.

Barnaby had taken one look and immediately understood the situation. He did his monkey maneuver, descending like lightning. Rosie looked down only once

97

and only briefly, to see that Barnaby was getting safely away. Then she turned her attention to the man above her.

He, too, was starting down, toward her, and he was almost as fast as Barnaby. She knew she'd never be able to outdistance him, and while the thought formed in her mind, he came even with her. His hairy arm went around her waist from behind and pulled her back against his sweaty chest. She felt his dampness through her shirt and shuddered with revulsion. His raw breath on her cheek made her stomach turn.

"Now, girl, ye aren't so brave, are ye?" The arm around her held the knife, while the other hand gripped the ropes.

Rosie couldn't decide which frightened her more, being stabbed to death in the rigging or falling to her death onto the deck or into the sea. The pulse of her blood sang in her ears and she wondered if that was the last sound she would ever hear.

Her fear of falling was so great that she wound her wrists into the ratlines for security and didn't even feel the ropes bite through her flesh. If he stabbed her up here, there was a possibility she could survive. But if he stabbed her and then she fell, she would have no chance.

The mechanics of using his knife while they were both trying to keep from falling seemed to baffle the man. He shifted the dagger in his hand, but couldn't manipulate it in the proper direction. Then he raised his hand until his clenched fist rubbed against her breast.

"I think I'll keep ye up here a while," he said, his breath making bile rise in her throat. He moved his hand against her breast again and she clenched her teeth to keep from crying. She refused to die sniveling. "No sense wasting an opportunity I ain't likely to get too often. Ye're clean, too."

Rosie tried to kick backward with one bare foot while the other clung to the ropes. She missed the man, but at least caused him to shift his position to avoid being struck. She kicked at him again, and again he had to move out of her way. Over and over she kicked until he removed his arm from around her waist, apparently deciding he needed to hold onto the shrouds with both hands. As soon as he released her, she kicked again, as hard as she could, this time connecting with his knee.

In slow motion, he leaned backward, so far backward she didn't know how he continued to hold on. Until finally, finally, he didn't. His hand peeled away from the lines beside her and with a long, undulating scream, he fell, hitting the gunwale and bouncing over it into the sea.

The force of the kick had torn Rosie's feet from their hold and she dangled in the air, her wrists twined into the ratlines holding her aloft. Blood trickled down her arms, and her shoulders felt as if they were being separated from her body.

She called out for help, but with her head tipped back as she hung, her voice went up into the sky and was torn away in the wind.

There was a rushing blackness behind her eyes as she tried without success to regain her footing and take the weight off her punished wrists and shoulders.

Her feet seemed miles below her and unresponsive to her commands to return to the ropes. The cruel lines around her wrists had flayed away the skin and stopped the circulation to her hands, which were cold and numb. She wanted to faint, to die, to somehow escape the awful pain. But she could only hang, and endure it. She had never been good at surrender.

Suddenly Baptiste and Big Tom were at her side.

"Nom de Dieu," Baptiste said, supporting her with

one strong arm. "I must cut these ropes. They've bitten so deeply I cannot unwind them."

Her head fell back against his shoulder, and the relief from the strain on her arms was beyond description.

"*Petite,* how did you become so entangled?"

"I did it," Rosie whispered. "I was so afraid of falling."

Baptiste made a rough sound in his throat as he cut the ropes, then ordered Big Tom to make temporary splices while, gently, he helped Rosie down to the deck. Afterward, she hardly remembered the descent, only her gratitude that Baptiste, strong Baptiste, was with her, supporting her, guiding her, murmuring to her in a language she couldn't understand.

She was going to have to revise her opinion of pirates. Nowhere in her categories of fool, cad or criminal could she accommodate this man.

Chapter 17

Rosie lay on Tuti's bunk, her arms flat at her sides, her wrists bound in white bandages. Under the bandages were the wounds Tuti had stitched and dressed with wet tea leaves and powdered alum to stop the bleeding.

Tuti had given her something to dull the pain and help her sleep, and she hung in a woozy state of semi-consciousness, breathing the clean fragrances of Tuti's herbs and spices while Tuti went off to tend the other wounded.

The sound of the door closing brought her closer to wakefulness.

"Rosie?" Barnaby asked. "Are you awake?"

She turned her head toward him and opened her eyes. "Hello, Barnaby. I can't tell. Tuti gave me something."

He stood beside her bed, worrying a length of rope in his dirty fingers. "Do your arms hurt bad?"

"Not yet. I'm too numb. But I'll wager they're going to. Are you all right?"

"Yes. But maybe I wouldn't be if you hadn't done what you did," he said, his sharp features solemn.

"I'm not sure I could have done it if I'd known how

it was going to turn out," Rosie said with a foggy smile, "so it probably doesn't count as real bravery."

"I guess you saved my life."

"Well, you sent Baptiste and Big Tom up to help me, so we're even. I just wish I'd learned how to get down out of the rigging as fast as you do. When I'm better you'll have to teach me." She was so weary she could hardly think. But she didn't want to worry Barnaby with her weakness, so she made an effort to seem alert.

"Sure." He stuck his hands in his pockets. "I didn't think a girl could be so brave."

That woke her up. "I'm surprised to hear you say that, Barnaby. You serve under a female captain. Don't you think Octavia could have done what I did?"

"Oh, aye," he said, "but she's different. Raider always says there's not another woman like her in the world."

"Oh, really," Rosie said, piqued. "What makes him such an expert? I'm sure there are lots of women as competent as Octavia."

"Raider's known lots of women," Barnaby said, relishing his knowledge. "He says one of the reasons his father sent him to sea when he was fourteen was to get his mind off his—oh." He hesitated. "Tuti probably wouldn't like it if I said that in front of you. She says she has a lot to undo to teach me some manners. But Raider also said that that's where most fourteen-year-old boys' minds are. He says you outgrow it. I want to be just like Raider, so I'm sure I'll be like that when I'm fourteen."

Rosie had seen enough boys like that at La Señora's to know what Barnaby meant. But she'd seen plenty of grown men the same way, with all their brains in their . . . well, whatever Barnaby had meant to say. "In spite of what your infallible Raider says, I don't see any reason why women can't rescue men. Heaven knows there's plenty they need rescuing from. But I won't ever save you again if you don't want me to.''

He squirmed and looked down at his toes. ''Oh, Rosie, don't be mad. I'm glad you did what you did. It just was strange, is all. I ain't sorry you did it.'' He withdrew one hand from his pocket and extended it to her. ''Here. I couldn't sleep last night, so I made this for you.''

Gingerly she raised one bandaged arm and took what he offered. It was a little carved kitten, curled into a ball, asleep.

''Oh, Barnaby, it's wonderful. And it looks just like Middy. Thank you very much.'' Noticing the more cheerful expression on his face, she went on. ''Now you must tell me all about the battle. We must have won, but I don't know anything else.''

''Oh, we won, for sure,'' he said with great enthusiasm. ''And not too many casualties, either. That's why Octavia hates a fight, you know. She hates for anybody to get hurt. But she doesn't shrink from one, neither. It's sometimes necessary, she says.'' He plopped himself down on the edge of the bunk and Rosie cautiously moved over as much as she could to avoid having her painful places jostled by him.

''Privateering seems an odd occupation for somebody who's bothered by fighting,'' Rosie said.

''That's so,'' Barnaby agreed, wiggling into a more comfortable position. ''That's why Raider made her bring Tuti, to fix the men who get hurt. But it's very important to her to find Raider's brother, so that's why we search every English ship we catch. This time wasn't too bad. We didn't take too many casualties, but we didn't find him on board, either, and that always makes her sad. We only lost one man, but they lost a lot.''

"The one we lost, who—?" She couldn't bear to think it might be one of the men she knew.

"Nobody you know. Toby Singleton." Barnaby shrugged as if it didn't matter. But he had to clear his throat before he could speak again. "He was unlucky."

"Poor Toby," she said, and meant it, even though she hadn't known Toby. "What about the crew of the other ship? And the ship? Did you sink it?"

"Sink it?" he asked, horrified. "Why would we sink a fine English merchantman loaded with goods when we can take it to New Orleans and sell the ship *and* the cargo for a big price? We all get a share of that, you know."

"No, I didn't know that," Rosie said. "So we'll be going to New Orleans now?"

"No!" he said, exasperated. "We put a prize crew aboard to sail it back. And some of the most wounded, too. We'll go on to The Cove short-handed." He held up his hand. "I know what you want to know next. You ask almost as many questions as me. The *White Swan*'s crew—that's the name of the merchantman, the *White Swan*—was put to sea in their small boats. We gave them maps and provisions. Not all privateers do that, but Octavia insists." He rolled his eyes at this feminine whim. "They'll find land soon. We're never far from it around here. They'll be all right. It was a good fight."

Rosie didn't think she believed in such a thing as a good fight.

"Baptiste said as soon as the deck's cleaned up—it's all dirty and bloody from the fight, you know—you can come topside and sit in the sun. The crew wants to meet you, anyway."

"Meet me? Why?"

"I don't know. I guess they're curious. You'll like

them. And you'll get used to the way they look after a while. And to their habits."

"What do you mean, the way they look? And their habits?"

"Well, they're rough, but that's the way sea dogs are. Like Max, the one who's teaching me to carve. His front teeth are out. And Animal has all those tattoos. And Octavia's always trying to get Big Tom to stop spitting, but he won't. Things like that. But none of them look near as bad as Nicodemus McNair, and you've seen him, so there's nothing to worry about. Right?"

"If you say so." Oh, she was tired. All she wanted now was some sleep.

Barnaby got off the bunk. "I better go. Tuti told me not to stay long. I'll come see you later." He turned away and just as he opened the door to leave, Rosie thought she heard him say, "Thanks," in a barely audible mumble.

Her dreams were crowded with images: her father falling over the bar at the Drop Anchor, his hand holding his chest; Raider's face seen through the smoke; the pitching deck of the *Ladyship* viewed from the top of the mast; Tuti smoking her pipe: all swirled and swept through her mind and made her sleep restless.

When she woke, she still felt tired and drugged, and Tuti was in the room, watching her.

"So, *bébé*, how do you feel now? It hurts, yes?"

"It hurts, yes," Rosie agreed. "Everything hurts." But, she realized, she really didn't mind. Since boarding the *Ladyship,* she'd been terrified, bewildered, bullied and wounded. But she'd also had more people answering more questions for her than ever before in her life. She'd been fussed over by Tuti as she'd always wanted someone to do. And she'd been inside adventures that made her feel alive as she never had in Campeche. As long as she stayed on the *Ladyship*, she knew there would be more adventures and more for her to learn. She liked the anticipation, and even the bit of fear that went with it.

"I will give you something to distract you," Tuti said. "You can go now onto the deck and meet the men. They are very curious about you."

"I think I'm curious about them, too," Rosie said.

Tuti laughed. "I wonder which of you will be the more surprised."

Chapter 18

Rosie sat on a low stool, her back against the capstan, her bandaged wrists resting in her lap, as Barnaby, flushed with importance, brought the members of the crew to meet her. The few of them who were left once the prize crew and the wounded had departed on the *White Swan* stood waiting, and Rosie felt, almost physically, the force of their eyes upon her. She looked right back at them.

Max, burly and swarthy, indeed had no front teeth. And he was so bashful, he was the only one who couldn't meet her eyes. Instead, he pressed into her unresisting hand a small carved ship, so exquisite in detail that each stay and halyard, brace and clew line, hung separately.

Rosie was very impressed with the delicate thing, particularly when contrasted with its maker. "Thank you," she told him. "It's very beautiful."

Big Tom squatted next to her to examine it. "Be nice if our own rigging was that size. Baptiste cut a considerable amount of rope to get you down, and there's almost nothing I hate more than splicing rope."

"I'm sorry I made work for you," Rosie said. "But I can't be sorry Baptiste did it."

He patted her head with his huge hand as if she were a pet, and she felt the clumsy thumps all the way through her drug-muddled brain. "Ah, well. Saving Barnaby was probably worth it. Though I don't always think so," he said, taking a swipe at Barnaby. "There's times I'd like to make fish food out of him."

Hastily, Barnaby beckoned to a sailor wearing no shirt. "Rosie, this is Animal. Ain't those tattoos something?"

On Animal's arms were strings of hearts, each one centered with a different woman's name. "I always like to be prepared," he told Rosie.

She read aloud: "Marie, Lucia, Annie, Monique, Addie, Elvoria—that one barely fits into the heart."

"She was a big girl, too," Animal said, chuckling at the memory.

A dancing girl covered Animal's chest, and at Barnaby's insistence, he showed a fascinated Rosie how he could make his tattoo dance by flexing his muscles. With more muscle flexing, an octopus undulated across his back. Rosie had seen anchors and flowers and such tattooed on sailors' forearms and biceps in the Drop Anchor, but never anything like this.

"Does it hurt very much to get tattooed?" she asked Animal. She didn't see how it could hurt any more than her wrists and shoulders did now.

"Naw. Just a little. You thinkin' of gettin' one? I knew a woman once in Galveston who had a butterfly on her . . . her . ." He stopped, unable to think of a decent euphemism. "It looked right nice," he finished.

Having a tattoo had never before occurred to Rosie, but now the thought of having a butterfly or maybe a seashell on her—somewhere—seemed quite in keeping with the new life she was embarked upon. She decided to ask Tuti about it later.

Next she met Tiny, the cook. He was a dwarf who

wiped his little hands on his greasy apron before extending one to Rosie and then quickly withdrew it when he saw how much it cost her in pain to raise her hand to his.

She'd never seen such a little man before and couldn't think what to say to him without mentioning his size, a subject about which she didn't know how sensitive he was. "You must fit perfectly in the galley," she finally said, deciding that anyone on a vessel like the *Ladyship* was probably tough enough to tolerate anything she might say.

"You're right," he said in an astonishingly deep and cultured voice. "But I can work even better in a big kitchen, with fresh food. You'll see when we get to The Cove. Salt beef and hardtack at sea aren't much of a challenge."

"The challenge is keeping the weevils from running off with the biscuits," Big Tom said, spitting over the side. "We got to bang them on the deck before we eat them, to knock the little buggers out."

Tiny looked indignant. "We have less weevils than any ship around. I heard some Brits talking once about how they ate in the dark so they wouldn't have to look at their wormy biscuits. And how their salt beef was so hard it could take a polish. We're not so bad off. At least we put in to The Cove now and again where we can eat well."

"Right you are, Tiny," Big Tom said. "And thank God for that. The best I can say about shipboard food is ain't nobody starved on the *Ladyship* yet. Though, Missy," he said, turning to Rosie, "you might be the first if you don't put some meat on them bones of yours."

"I'll make her up something special," Tiny said.

"What you got that's special that you ain't giving us?" Animal asked. The hearts on his bare arms gave him a festive appearance, in contrast to the growl of his voice.

"Nothing today," Tiny said. "But tomorrow, when we go ashore for Tuti to get some of her weeds and seeds, I guarantee you I can find something to make a feast."

At this point Baptiste arrived, carrying a small barrel and a dipper. "A good time for grog, I think," he said, setting down the barrel.

"What's grog?" asked Rosie, who knew only rum, ale and *x-tabentum*.

"It's rum and water," Baptiste said. "A ration a day is usual, but today I think we have earned more." He ladled dipperfuls into the tin cups the sailors extended to him. He put half a ladle into an extra cup and handed it to Rosie. "For you, *petite*," he said. "You have earned it as much as we." He lifted his cup toward the knot of sailors around Rosie and said, "Well done. The *White Swan* is a fine prize." He paused for a moment and added, "We will not forget Toby Singleton. *Bois sec.*"

Solemnly the men drank, and Rosie raised her cup, too. The grog burned in her throat, and she could feel it all the way down to her stomach. Her eyes watered and she clenched her teeth to keep from coughing. Strangely, after a moment, she didn't seem to feel the pain in her wrists and shoulders as much. She took another drink.

"What does *bois sec* mean?" Rosie asked.

"*Bois sec* is 'drink dry,' " Baptiste said, refilling the cups. "But you see, they need no encouragement."

The sailors sat on the deck, their cups in their hands, enjoying their moment of leisure in the company of the surprising visitor.

Rosie saw that Barnaby, too, had a cup of grog in his hand, and a vainglorious look on his face. She almost said something about the appropriateness of rum as a beverage for ten-year-old boys, but thought better of it. Instead, she took another sip of her own grog.

Noticing her shudder, Baptiste laughed and said,

"Stay with us awhile, *petite,* and we will have you drinking Blackbeard's favorite—rum mixed with gunpowder. A drink for a real pirate."

"I don't see how that could taste any stronger than this," Rosie said. "I might as well try it right now."

Baptiste laughed his mirthful laugh and touched his cup to hers. "*Oui,*" he said. "You would make an excellent pirate. Fearless and eager. Laffite could use you."

Rosie took another drink. Her arms felt much better now, and she had a sudden, odd urge to sing.

"Come on, Wolf," Barnaby said, tugging at the arm of a tall, slender Indian boy with shoulder-length black hair and a stern, high-cheekboned face. "You have to meet Rosie, too."

"Hello, Wolf," Rosie said as Wolf stared impassively back at her. "I'm happy to meet you." She was. She was happy to meet them all. Somehow she no longer felt like the misfit she had always considered herself in Campeche. How could she, among a crew that included a dwarf, a tattooed man, a *traiteur,* a ten-year-old boy, a woman captain and heaven knew what else? It didn't bother her in the slightest that Wolf only nodded almost imperceptibly to her and went to hunker silently at the back of the group.

Barnaby introduced her to Mickey, a sixteen-year-old redhead with a sunburned, freckled face, and to Luke, a lanky boy with arms that seemed longer than they should be, and hands as big as buckets. Then they sat, drinking their grog, and Rosie watched the sailors, her head light and throbbing, a giddy smile on her face.

"Come," Baptiste said. "We must teach our Rosie some ways of the sea. We must each give her some bits of wisdom we have learned if she is to become a proper pirate. Big Tom, what have your years before the mast taught you?"

"This is everything I know," Big Tom said, and began to sing a favorite sailor's jingle, accompanying himself with his fiddle: "Six days shalt thou labor, as hard as thou art able. On the seventh, scrub the deck and scrape the cable."

There were shouts of agreement from the other sailors when he finished, and Rosie clapped her hands, though the rhyme's uneven meter bothered her. Big Tom continued to scrape softly on his fiddle, a pleasant accompaniment to the conversation.

"Now Animal," Baptiste said, pointing with his empty cup. "And have a little care. Her ears are not pirate's ears yet."

Rosie was feeling unaccountably pleased at the thought of becoming a pirate.

"Well," said Animal, thinking hard. "I know. I can tell you what a son of a gun is. It's a young'un conceived by a sailor and a fancy woman on the gun deck of a ship. Them British captains are so afraid their sailors'll desert, they won't let 'em off ship in a good port. Instead, they bring the women on board."

Rosie had enough rum in her to have forgotten whatever maidenly diffidence she might have possessed. She listened, spellbound and saucer-eyed.

"That will do quite well, and quite enough," Baptiste said. "Max?"

Max shook his head and looked at the deck. "Nah," he muttered.

"Please, Max," Rosie begged, her curiosity inflamed. "You must know a lot of interesting things."

"Well, I do know a story," he began, his eyes still lowered, his words blurred by his lack of front teeth. "About how bad the British navy is. This is why those sailors desert in the good ports. In the bad ones, too, for that matter. Well, there was this deserter from a British ship. Somehow, he got taken aboard the U.S.

frigate *Essex*." Max's voice gained volume if not clarity as he told his story. "His first officer come right after him, and the Americans, well, they had to let him go. They all knew he was goin' to a floggin' or worse, but they had to." He took a quick look at Rosie's face and then lowered his head again. "This sailor, see, he asked to go below for his things, and he went right to the carpenter's bench and chopped off his left hand."

Rosie gasped.

"Then he come topside and throwed it at the first officer's feet and said he'd cut off his left foot before he'd go back to the Royal Navy."

Grimacing, Rosie asked, "What happened to him?"

He sneaked another quick look at her. "They left him on the *Essex*. They already got too many crippled English sailors."

"What could be worse than a flogging?" Rosie asked, appalled by her terrible curiosity, but not appalled enough to keep from asking the question.

Voices clamored to answer her. The men were as interested as she was, it seemed, in the diversities of cruelty.

"There's rubbin' vinegar and gunpowder in the wounds after a floggin' to make them hurt more," Mickey volunteered.

"There's cuttin' a man to death," Luke said, "by hacking off a little piece of him at a time."

"There's woolding," Barnaby piped up, "where you tie a cord around somebody's neck and tighten it by twisting a stick until his eyes pop out."

"I don't believe that," Rosie said.

"Nor I," Baptiste said. "Enough, *mes amis*. You will give our poor *petite* bad dreams. I will tell you of Blackbeard, who had fourteen wives in fourteen ports and kept them all happy. And how he twisted ropes into his beard and lit them before boarding a ship he had attacked, to frighten his foes with his flaming face. Once, when he was full of rum and gunpowder, he took his mates into the hold with him, sealed the hatches and lit pots of brimstone. He stayed there longer than all the others, even though he was almost suffocated, and he laughed when he came up. When he was finally caught, it took twenty cutlass wounds and five pistol balls to kill him. A man of great style, *oui*?"

"*Oui*," Rosie repeated, dazzled.

Tuti, who had been standing at the back of the group watching and saying nothing, finally spoke. "I must now have back my patient. She needs to rest. Come, *bébé*. Baptiste is right. You will have bad dreams."

Reluctantly Rosie stood up, and had to reach out to the capstan for support, her head was spinning so. Baptiste took her elbow to steady her. "Thank you for the stories," she said. "I never had a better time."

"Shame on you, Baptiste," Tuti scolded, pushing through the men to shepherd Rosie to the companion-way. "Fill her with rum and scare her to death."

"While you watched and listened, too," Baptiste reminded her, his dark eyes shining. "And I do not think she seems so very frightened."

"She needs to know a little at a time," Tuti said, starting Rosie down the steps. "Not everything at once."

Suddenly exhausted, Rosie was halfway down the steps when she heard a male voice, she couldn't tell whose, say, "How can a female who looks like that, with that shape, put me in mind of my little sister? Have I been at sea so long I've forgotten how to be a man?"

"Did you ever know?" someone else said, and the laughter followed Rosie all the way to Tuti's cabin and filled her dreams, none of which were bad.

Chapter 19

The next day the *Ladyship* anchored for the afternoon at a small, uninhabited island where Tuti had previously found particular healing herbs she needed to supplement her stores.

The men, granted a few hours off while Tuti gathered her herbs, piled into longboats and went ashore; there they swam, climbed trees, slept on the sunny beach and generally acted like boys playing truant.

Octavia wouldn't leave her ship, and Rosie was too tired to, not even considering the distressing headache she'd had all day—from the grog, Tuti scolded—and the acute pain in her wrists. The two of them found themselves sitting together on the quarterdeck, watching the men ashore like doting mothers.

"That was a very brave thing you did for Barnaby," Octavia said after they had sat in silence for a long time, almost paralyzed by the sun and the rocking motion of the *Ladyship*.

"Oh, no," Rosie said. "I was terrified the whole time."

"That shows only that you've got good sense. People who aren't afraid are those too stupid to understand the situation. True courage is doing what you must even when you're terrified.''

"Do you mean you're afraid when you go into battle?" Rosie thought Octavia had seemed supremely confident and courageous on the eve of the fight with the *White Swan*.

"Every time," Octavia said.

"And you keep doing it?"

Octavia inclined her head. "It never gets easier. But I can't stop."

"Why not?" Rosie knew she would never have gone into the rigging after Barnaby unless she'd had no choice.

"Because what I do is right. So I must not stop. The British have interfered too much with our shipping rights, and with our freedom at sea. Impressment is a terrible thing. No seaman is safe. The English must accept that America is sovereign now. The Revolution is over; they must leave us alone. Have you seen the banner 'Free Trade and Sailors' Rights' on any of the ships in the harbor at Campeche?"

Rosie shook her head. "I never noticed," she said, feeling woefully uninformed and unobservant.

"That's what this war is about, though not all Americans wanted it, to be sure. I align myself with Clay and Calhoun, the war hawks. John Randolph is against them, but who can care what a man thinks who never takes off his spurs, brings his favorite hound into the House and drinks porter all day?" She gave Rosie a sidelong glance. "Raider feels as I do."

Rosie had never felt so ignorant. And for once in her life, she couldn't think of a single question to ask.

At Rosie's silence, Octavia continued. "Did you know Raider's brother has been impressed?"

"Yes. Tuti told me. Did you know him?"

"Yes," she said. "Very well."

Rosie waited, but Octavia didn't continue. So she said, "Finding him seems almost impossible. He could be anywhere, couldn't he?"

Octavia nodded. "Anywhere or nowhere. We know many impressed Americans have been sent to Dartmoor, the English prison, because they refused to cooperate aboard British ships. And we know many have died there." Her voice was very low.

"So you don't even know if he's still alive?"

"We don't know. And sometimes I don't believe he is." She paused, thinking. "Raider would never say that. But it makes him all the more intent on vengeance against Charles Lawrence." The way Octavia said that name was as if the very words had a bad taste to them.

"Raider must be sad," Rosie said. She knew she would be if she'd ever been lucky enough to have a brother and he was lost. Though, come to think of it, she hadn't seen any signs of sadness in Raider.

Octavia looked at Rosie sharply and then looked away, smoothing her white skirt over her knees. "Yes. And angry. And guilty."

"Guilty? Why guilty?"

"Because he's still alive and free, while his brother isn't. May not be," she amended. "They were on the same ship when Lawrence attacked. He left Raider and others for dead and took the rest of the crew."

"But that wasn't Raider's fault," Rosie said, inexplicably coming to his defense. "He must have been terribly wounded to be left for dead."

"He was," Octavia said, her mouth set grimly.

The bright tropical sun was heading for the horizon when the first longboat returned with Tuti and her filled baskets. As she climbed up the rope ladder, she saw Rosie and Octavia together and came over to join them.

"How do you feel, *bébé*?" she asked Rosie.

Rosie hardly knew what to say. Her wrists hurt. Her shoulders and her head hurt, too. And something else hurt—something inside, in an indefinable place, hurt for a young man she barely knew and who had done her great harm; an angry, sad and guilty young man.

"I have a headache," she finally said.

"Still? I am not surprised," Tuti said briskly. "Drinking rum and listening to stories of horror all yesterday afternoon. Come with me below and I will make you tea for what hurts you."

Rosie didn't believe there was such a tea, but she rose to follow Tuti. Then she turned back to Octavia and said, "If there's anything I can ever do . . . I don't know what it might be, but if there is . . . to help . . . or—or anything . . ." She felt foolish even as she said it. Whatever could she do to help someone like Octavia?

Octavia smiled at her, only a small smile, but it made her already exquisite face still lovelier. "Thank you," she said. "I appreciate that. And so would Raider."

Flushed with the pleasure of Octavia's approval, Rosie had taken only a few steps toward the hatch when she almost ran into Wolf, who had appeared so silently she hadn't heard him.

"Oh, Wolf, excuse me. I was thinking of something else."

Without a word, he handed her a spray of small white orchids with golden throats.

"Why, thank you," she said as she took them. "They're beautiful. They make me wish I'd gone ashore to see where they grow."

He touched her lightly on one bandaged wrist and then on one shoulder and vanished as silently as he'd appeared.

Rosie sighed. Another male she couldn't fit into her categories.

Tuti was laying out the tea things when Rosie came

into the cabin, and the smell of fresh herbs was heady in the small space. In the middle of the table was a bouquet of wildflowers in one of Tuti's green glass bottles, and a piece of fruit that was unfamiliar to Rosie.

Tuti gestured to the flowers and the fruit. "For you." Before Rosie could thank her, she added, "Not from me. From Mickey. He asked me to give them to you."

"Well," Rosie said, astonished. She held the branch of orchids out to Tuti. "Wolf brought me these."

"Wolf, too? So. You see, I am right, am I not? Something new begins now."

"But what is it? What's beginning?" Rosie asked, putting the orchids into the same bottle with the wildflowers.

"It is better for you to understand that for yourself. You will."

"I wouldn't be so sure of that," Rosie said, sitting down at the table and looking at her flowers. "There's a lot I don't understand. I always try, but— My father used to tell me I'd never be smart, that I'd always be like his sister, Polly, who couldn't do anything but sew. We lived with her when I was little, before my mother died, but I don't really remember her. And then he wanted to leave me with her when he moved on after Mother died. But she was ill and couldn't take care of me, so he had to take me with him, though I always knew he didn't want to. He should have been glad he had me. I learned to read and write better than he ever could, and I ran the business from the time I was twelve. He said that was something like a trick, that it didn't count as real smartness." Remembering was not a good thing to do when she already hurt so much.

"He was cruel and a fool, and ignorant of your heart," Tuti said fiercely. "He was not the correct father for you. I am sure he said many words that hurt you."

Rosie looked down at the table to hide the quick flow of tears. How strange that echoes of words from years ago could make her cry when her fresh and painful physical wounds had not.

"They are all untrue," Tuti said. "All. I will tell you the true ones. He was blind to your beauty without and within."

Rosie raised her head, her thick lashes wet and spiked from tears. "I'm not—"

Tuti cut her off. "You are," she said harshly. And then, more softly, "You are. And part of that beauty is that you do not know it. Listen to me only. And to the men of this ship. They are rough, but Octavia has chosen them partly because they can see with their hearts."

Rosie couldn't think now. The recent events plus the memories of her father left her too exhausted to do more than shrug.

"I will bring your tea, and then you must sleep," Tuti said.

Chapter 20

Sleep she did, until Tiny himself brought her dinner and stood by while she woke and washed and finally tasted his offering.

"It's dove," he told her. "Max snared them and told me to fix the fattest ones for you. How do you like them?"

"They're wonderful," she said. She wasn't being polite; they *were* wonderful, in spite of being so full of tiny bones—tender and highly seasoned.

"Not too hot?" he asked. "The men like things spicy. It helps disguise the taste of—never mind."

"I like spicy food," Rosie said, swallowing. "I'm used to *achiote* and sour orange and *habañero chiles,* you know. It's hard to make something too hot for me."

"The only one I can't get food too hot for is Raider. The man must have iron pipes."

"Sometime, make me something as hot as you do for him," Rosie said. "Just so I can see what it's like."

"You're not going to like it," he warned her.

"I'm curious," she said. "Humor me. You can laugh if I explode."

"All right," Tiny said dubiously. "I'd never laugh, but you're not going to like it."

*   *   *

Rosie spent much of the next few days sitting on the sunny deck, resting and healing, while the men of the crew missed no opportunity to stop beside her for a word or, when they had the time, a longer visit. Max and Barnaby often sat beside her, Barnaby chattering away, bragging or teasing, Max silent as they worked on their carvings. She'd always taken such pleasure in watching her embroidered designs grow; now she derived the same contentment from watching the carved ships and animals take shape.

Animal showed her how to make designs with knots, though she couldn't actually do it because tying the rope hurt her wrists. When she asked him what he was making, he only said, "You'll see."

One midday, when she sat absorbing the healing sun and watching Max carve, Tiny brought a kettle of stew on deck to serve lunch picnic-style. The stew was made from fresh-caught fish and onions and dried vegetables. And spices; lots and lots of spices.

"Christ, Tiny, are you trying to kill us?" Big Tom asked, tears streaming from his eyes after he'd taken a bite. "What did you put in here?"

"Rosie wanted to try something as hot as Raider likes it," Tiny said. "So I made this."

"Well, do something to fix it. This'll burn out her innards and set fire to her chemise."

Rosie giggled. "My innards are used to hot food," she said. "And my chemise is fireproof. Let me have some."

The stew was hot, all right. Hot enough to make her eyes water and her nose run. But it was good, too, and she wasn't one of those who measured how good a dish was by how much it hurt.

Well, she thought stoutly as she ate the stew, if this

is as hot as Captain Raider Lyons can take it, I'm as much of a man as he.

After lunch, she left her wheezing, weepy-eyed companions to go below and talk to Tuti about a tattoo.

"So you like the look of Animal's tattoos, do you?" Tuti asked. "And he told you about the woman in Galveston with the tattoo on her derriere?"

"Is *that* where it was?"

"Is that not what Animal said?"

"He just said it was *on* her." Musing, she said, "I wonder if that was Elvoria. He seemed happy to remember her."

"Animal is happy to remember all of them."

"How many woman does a man need, anyway?" Rosie was as curious as she was indignant. "Why isn't one enough?"

"*Bébé*, sit down." Tuti pulled out Rosie's chair. "I will make us some tea and we will have a talk about men and women. I think you need to know about that much more than you need to know about tattoos. And I see I will be the one to tell you. How lucky for you."

Rosie sat at the table like an obedient student, every nerve alert. At last she was going to get some answers about something vital.

Tuti made tea, brought it to the table and sat in the chair opposite Rosie. She put her small brown hands over Rosie's. "I understand you have a poor opinion of men because of your odious father and the men you have seen in the work you have had to do. But there are other kinds. I have told you I will be truthful with you always, and I am being so now. If a man—a good man, you understand—has the right woman, he needs only one. From her he gets love and companionship and talking and laughing and good fighting and wonderful lovemaking. But, *bébé*, this is rare. So men go to other women for these things and at home they have respectability and children."

"But why would a man marry someone he knows won't give him the things he needs?" Rosie asked. "And what about what a woman needs?"

"Those are good questions," Tuti said. "You ask many good questions. There is no other way to learn."

Percy had always said her inquisitiveness was offensive, as if he would even *know* what was offensive. Now it came to her that perhaps he had done so because he was unable to answer her questions.

She didn't expect she'd ever understand why her beautiful Portuguese mother had married him. Maybe what Tuti had to tell her would help to explain it.

"Men marry because it is expected," Tuti said. "Or from infatuation. Or false impressions. Marriage is a convenience for some men; they do not necessarily expect to find love in a marriage. Love is not a requirement in a convenience. For myself, I had to have love. I could never have married for convenience."

"Have you a husband?" Rosie asked. For some reason, she'd never thought of Tuti as a wife. Perhaps because she seemed so content by herself, with her own life. And what man would like having his wife off at sea for months at a time?

"Not now. But I have had. Three of them."

"Three!" Rosie couldn't think of having even one. "What happened to them?"

"Two died. One decided he loved someone else more than me and he left. I did not like it, of course. But I had a life outside of him, and my work, and I have found other men to love. No more marriages; I am too old for that. Too old to learn about another man." She gave Rosie a glinting look of mischief. "Unless he is a special man, of course."

Then she became more serious. "I know how to love

because I am Cajun. Many good women think it is wrong to give a man the things he needs—especially the laughing and the wonderful lovemaking. I am talking about English women, American women. Not Cajun women; they think differently. But English and American women, they are brought up to think this way. A woman needs the same things a man needs, the very same things. But many women, these English and American women, do not know they need it, so they cannot even look for it. So sad. And they do not know that when they give it, it comes back to them.''

"So that's why men have a lot of women? And women like La Señora's ladies?''

"Yes. They are looking for the *wonderful* part of being with a woman. With wives they find duty and order and children and respect and community. But *wonderful* is often somewhere else—the love and the laughing and perhaps even the talking. How much nicer to have it at home.'' Her dark eyes glinted again. ''And less expensive.''

"Tuti,'' Rosie began, then stopped.

"*Oui, bébé?* Go on. You can ask,'' Tuti reassured her.

She took a deep breath and plunged. ''What *is* wonderful lovemaking?''

Tuti looked at her. ''How much do you know of the way men and women are together?''

Rosie studied her hands. ''The basics, I suppose. But not from personal experience,'' she added hastily. ''La Señora's ladies didn't say much about what they did except to make fun of the men who came to see them.''

Tuti laughed, thoroughly amused. ''*Eh, bien,* so I will tell you. It will make more sense when you have had some experience, but ...'' and she went on to explain the details of how physical love was conducted.

Two bright pink spots appeared on Rosie's cheeks

and her mouth half opened in disbelief. When Tuti used French words, Rosie had to stop her and make her translate, and when Tuti couldn't make her message clear in English, she brought out paper and pen and drew pictures. Rosie's pink spots grew bigger.

Finally, Tuti sat back in her chair and said, "*Eh bien*. There are yet more variations, but I think you have heard enough for now. So what have you to say about your new knowledge?"

After a silence, Rosie asked, "Are you sure about this?"

Tuti burst into a rush of her hoarse laughter. When she could speak again, she said, "Oh, poor *bébé*. By the time I was your age, I had had some experience and the idea no longer seemed preposterous to me. In fact, I had already learned, with my first husband, that when there is love, it can be a splendid thing." Seeing the look on Rosie's face, she added, "You will think so, too, one day, believe it or not. I know what you say about men, but has there not been some man, sometime in your life, whom you can think of a little this way?"

Rosie dipped her head and stared into her untouched cup of tea, her cheeks burning. What little she knew about physical desire she had learned at the moment Raider Lyons's mouth met hers on the deck of the *Ladyship*.

"Ah," Tuti said, patting Rosie's hand.

"What about love?" Rosie asked, still looking into her teacup. "What about that?"

"Oh, yes, *l'amour*. Love is a strange thing. It cannot be helped; it cannot be summoned; it cannot be ignored. It comes whether you are ready for it or not, whether you want it or not, whether it is a good time for it or not. And when it comes, it is a gift. Take it."

But Rosie didn't want it, gift or no. She wanted her old feelings back, where men fit into categories and where all she desired was a tidy life of sewing and her animals and adopted children. Yet she knew those feelings were gone for good, the way the rest of her life in Campeche was.

As Tuti leaned toward her, a question on her face, they heard, shouted so loudly from the deck that the sound carried down the passage and through the closed door, "A sail! A sail!"

Chapter 21

Rosie jumped up from her chair and followed Tuti along the companionway.

The sail was off on the horizon, a small, dark triangle that seemed to grow larger by the instant as the *Ladyship*, close-hauled, bore down on it. Rosie and Tuti stood at the rail, watching, as the too-small crew hastened into readiness, the way it had before taking the *White Swan*.

The distance between the two ships continued to close, and Rosie felt a quiver of fear as they neared the other ship. Would she somehow again be drawn to do something dangerous, something that frightened her, something she never would have predicted she would do? There was no way she could know, and it made her feel a stranger to herself, yet, oddly, as if she were just beginning to learn who she was and what she could do.

When everything was ready, Octavia and the men came to stand by the rail, too, and watch, puzzled, as the other ship made no attempt to outrun them. There was no sign at all of any activity aboard. The ship's sails appeared to be flapping aimlessly in the wind, unreefed and uncleated, and it wallowed in the sea, taking waves broadside and heeling sloppily.

"Is there no one at the helm?" Octavia asked.

Baptiste raised the glass to his eye. "I cannot see yet. Wait. Ah—no. I see no one. No one aloft, no one at the wheel."

"It's *Lightning*, isn't it?" Octavia asked, a tense urgency in her voice.

"Oui." Baptiste adjusted the glass. "There are bodies on the deck."

"Bodies? Let me see." She took the glass from him as the others gazed tensely across the water, trying to discern what lay aboard the ship they all both dreaded and anticipated meeting. Octavia looked for a long time before she lowered the glass, a crease between her perfect brows. "What can have happened? I see no blood. Is it plague? Poison?"

"Or a trick," Baptiste said. "Lawrence does them well."

"Look at the sails," Octavia said. "*Lightning* can't last long in these latitudes with her sails loose. Lawrence wouldn't take such a chance with his ship."

"Why should the sails be loose," Baptiste asked, "if it is plague? Or poison? And if it is plague, we are foolish to think of boarding. Worse than foolish—we are insane."

Octavia pressed her forefinger against her lips and thought. "How could Lawrence know it would be us who found him?"

"Why would he care *who* finds him? The fact that it is us is a wonderful accident for him."

"Listen to Baptiste," Big Tom said to Octavia. "You're captain, I know that, but you've always heard what the rest of us thought. I don't like the smell of it. We know there's a company of Royal Marines aboard the *Lightning*. Why don't we see any of their bodies?"

By now the *Ladyship* had come close enough so that they all could see the motionless bodies lying on the *Lightning*'s deck. Indeed, none of them appeared to be Royal Marines, only common seamen.

"A ghost ship?" Max murmured.

The failing light of the tropical evening gave an air of unreality to the silent ship. The wind had diminished, as it always did at twilight, and the two great ships drifted together, within hearing of the creak of each other's timbers.

"Not a good time to be so close if it's a trick," Big Tom told Octavia. "We have no wind."

"And they have no sails," she retorted.

"Lawrence, if he had a mind to, could get those men to square the yards even if they *were* dead."

"Big Tom is right," Baptiste said. "This is not a good spot we are in."

The sky slowly darkened and as they stood at the rail, watching and listening, a few tropical stars burned into the purple night sky.

Rosie looked up at the *Ladyship*'s sails, a pyramid of canvas so high above her it seemed as if the masts almost could touch those stars. The light breath of what wind there was could barely keep the sails distended.

"What if someone you cared for was on that ship?" Octavia asked. Her white clothing and flaxen hair seemed to gather the fading light and radiate it back. "What if it was me? Or Raider? Or ... or Raider's brother? As it may be. Would you still sail away?"

No one answered her.

"Or would you be willing to take a risk to find out?" she asked into the silence.

"I do not like it," Baptiste said, watching the *Lightning* yaw and wallow.

"I don't like it, either," Octavia said. "And I agree, it may be a trap. But if there's a chance we can find—"

Her voice caught, and Rosie was struck by how much Octavia must love Raider if she cared so much about finding his brother. "If we can find," Octavia continued, "the man we've been looking for for so long, I think we must take it."

"We are short-handed as it is," Baptiste reminded her.

She didn't reply, but raised the glass again. "Light the deck lanterns," she said.

With no lights aboard the *Lightning* or the *Ladyship,* it was becoming more and more difficult to see anything.

"We should do this in daylight," Baptiste said, resigned, apparently, to what Octavia wanted, but still trying to gain what advantage he could for the *Ladyship*.

"There's still light enough," she said. "But we must hurry. Get ready to come alongside and board."

Animal edged next to Rosie at the rail as the other men dispersed to light the lanterns and prepare for the boarding, and said softly to her, "Remember when you asked me what I was makin' and I told you you'd see? Well, it's these. I want you to have them, just in case." From his pocket he took something and pressed it into Rosie's hands.

"What is it?" she asked. "It's too dark to see."

"It's bracelets. Knotted ones to cover up them scars you have on your wrists. Them be bad ones and they won't be goin' away."

"Oh, Animal." Her eyes misted with tears and she touched his hard arm. Even in the dark she could imagine the tattooed hearts on it. "Thank you. I'll wear them forever."

She could barely see him as he ducked his head and moved his bulky shoulders uncomfortably. "Well. Maybe not forever," he muttered.

"Yes, forever," she vowed. "I'll never take them off."

"I best go," he said, not moving.

"Be careful. Don't do anything too brave or too foolish." She clutched the bracelets in her two hands and felt their knots under her fingers.

He chuckled. "I'm never too brave, but I sure have been too foolish." He moved away from her.

"Take care," she called after him.

She wished she could go with him. She hated being left out, even though the thought of boarding the *Lightning* and walking among those dead bodies made her shiver. Octavia would go, whether she was afraid or not.

But nobody's actually told me not to go, Rosie thought. What if something happens to all the rest of them? Do I really want to be left here alone? I wouldn't have the first idea how to sail this ship by myself, so I'd likely drown, anyway. And what if they were to find Raider's brother? Could I stand to miss such a wonderful moment?

She shoved the bracelets into the pockets of Tuti's let-down skirt and tried to be inconspicuous. She knew that if Tuti, overprotective as she was, gave a thought to her, she'd probably lock her up in the cabin. Rosie could only hope that Tuti was too preoccupied to wonder what she was up to.

The *Ladyship* came alongside the *Lightning* and the hulls thumped together, groaning. As soon as they touched, Big Tom and Max were throwing grappling hooks to bind the two ships. Once the hooks were set, instead of swarming aboard the *Lightning,* as they would have done for any other ship, the men clustered together, listening.

Nothing but ships' timbers rubbing and complaining. No shouts. No questions.

What had happened on the *Lightning*?

The *Ladyship* was bright with yellow lantern light, but the British frigate lurked in shadow, silent, mysterious and menacing. The unmoving white shirts of the sailors lying on the deck made the only interruptions in the gloom.

Octavia threw one leg over the *Ladyship*'s gunwale and then scrambled across to the deck of the *Lightning*.

"Someone hand me a lantern," she said.

Baptiste passed one across to her and then followed it himself. The *Ladyship* felt abandoned and alien with both Baptiste and Octavia gone from it. Rosie wanted to rush across to the *Lightning*'s deck to be with them again, but she knew her best chance was to wait and join the confusion when the rest of the crew went across.

She looked around her and saw her friends, even Tiny and Barnaby and Tuti, tensed and fully armed, their eyes glowing with some feral anticipation, focused on Octavia and Baptiste.

Octavia knelt beside the first crew member she came to. Baptiste stood over her, his pistol ready. She touched her hand to the man's cheek, then felt his neck for a pulse. Raising her head, she called, "He's dead."

"From what, can you tell?" Big Tom called back from the *Ladyship*.

"I don't know," Octavia said. "There doesn't seem to be any blood."

Baptiste, meanwhile, turned over another body with his booted foot. He wrinkled his nose. "This one's been dead for a while."

"But where's the rest of them?" Max asked through his missing teeth. "Is this like the *Flyin' Dutchman*? Everybody gone and no one knows how?"

"Let's go find out," Big Tom said. "I ain't too comfortable having the two of them over there alone." He pushed himself over the side and onto the *Lightning*'s deck. Everyone but Tuti and Tiny followed, including Rosie.

Darkness and confusion were not enough cover for her, however. She should have known Tuti would see her.

"Bébé!" Tuti commanded. "Where are you going? Return this moment!"

Rosie kept going, calling over her shoulder, "I'll be all right. I promise."

"You do not know enough to make such a promise," Tuti yelled, pressed against the gunwale and reaching out for Rosie, who had already made it over to the *Lightning*.

"It's all right," Rosie called. "Everybody's dead here. I'll be back as soon as I've looked around just a little. Don't worry. Everybody else is here and they're armed to the eyeballs. What can happen to me?"

Chapter 22

As Rosie said that, all the hatch covers on the deck flew open and crashed back against the deck planking. In the light of Octavia's single lamp, she saw a flood of Royal Marines come pouring forth, pistols and sabers drawn.

She heard shots but didn't know who had fired them, and when she turned to retreat to the *Ladyship,* she found her way blocked by a brace of Royal Marines stationed between her and Tuti.

How could they have gotten there so fast? Turning back to the *Lightning,* Rosie could hardly tell what was happening. The deck was a dark turmoil of struggling bodies and wavering shadows.

She couldn't go back and she was afraid to go forward. All she could do was to crouch, hugging her elbows, and watch, conscious for the first time in an hour of the ache in her wrists. Someone lit more lamps and in their light Rosie could clearly see how seriously outnumbered the crew of the *Ladyship* was.

Her heart thudded in her chest and she wondered how she could have been so stupid as to assure Tuti that nothing would happen to her because everyone on board was dead. It was beginning to look as if she and the crew of the *Ladyship* might be the dead ones.

In a matter of minutes, as was inevitable from the beginning, it was over.

Octavia struggled in the grip of two Royal Marines while Charles Lawrence stood beside the bow cannon, one hand resting lightly on the top of it, his other hand holding a long pistol pointed at Octavia's heart.

The crew of the *Ladyship* stood in a cluster, silent and powerless, as the *Lightning*'s men took their weapons from them. The Royal Marines who stood between Rosie and Tuti took Rosie by the arms and dragged her to stand with the crew. She was too frightened even to struggle, and cursed herself for her cowardice and her trembling limbs when Octavia still fought so hard, though escape was clearly impossible.

Somehow, standing with Big Tom and Baptiste, Max and Animal and Barnaby, Mickey and Wolf, in spite of the many guns trained on them all, made her feel a little better. Preferable to be in a bad spot with good company than alone, although she couldn't say why it made any difference.

She was disconcerted by the silence and stillness of the *Ladyship*'s men until she realized it wasn't the guns Lawrence's men trained on all of them that kept them immobilized. Under other circumstances they would have appreciated the challenge and relished the odds. No, it was the knowledge that any sudden movements from them could cause Octavia's death.

Rosie felt that pressure, too, and stood, stiff and frightened, her bloodless fingers biting into Barnaby's shoulders for support. She was flooded with renewed admiration for Octavia, whose expression showed no trace of fear, only outrage.

"I appear to have all the bargaining points," Lawrence remarked, satisfaction in every syllable. "Shall we begin?"

"I can't think what meaning a bargain would have to you," Octavia said coldly. "Nor how I might have anything to bargain with. You'll only take what you want."

He smiled silkily. "To be sure. I can take what I want. How easily will you give it to me?"

"What choice have I?" she asked. "I believe in a fair fight. I don't believe in suicide, and I won't sacrifice my crew in a hopeless contest."

"So," he said, an edge of disappointment to his words, "you'll simply give me what I want? That easily?"

Octavia's gaze met his in silence.

"Anything?" he asked.

Until that moment, Rosie had had her doubts that Lawrence could be as bad as Tuti, Baptiste, Octavia and Big Tom said he was. She'd wondered if they hadn't somehow misunderstood his motives, his intentions, that he'd only been doing what a responsible officer would do in a war, and that he intended them no personal malice. But now she saw in his face a sort of mad satisfaction, a vicious pleasure, that verified everything she'd been told.

Watching Octavia, Rosie realized how much strength and dignity silence could convey.

A vagrant breeze caused the sails of the *Lightning* to flap noisily, and fluttered the edges of Rosie's *tignon,* stirring the loose dark curls around her face. That small movement brought Charles Lawrence's gaze to her, and when she read the recognition and purpose in it, she looked away in terror. She suspected now what he meant to take from the *Ladyship.*

"There's but one thing I want," Lawrence said. "One thing only. Then you can sail away, to meet me another day, under more equal circumstances. It's your Captain Lyons I'd prefer to meet, besides.''

Rosie raised her head in time to see Octavia's eyes open fractionally in surprise. Rosie's hands tightened on Barnaby's shoulders until he flinched and yelped. The sound caused all eyes to turn to him. And to Rosie.

Captain Lawrence gave her a smile of such languid assurance that she shuddered and dropped her hands to her sides.

''Yes, my dear,'' he said to her, past the startled men of both ships.

Rosie's gaze was captured by his, but in her peripheral vision she saw Octavia turn toward her and lean in her direction, causing the Royal Marines holding each of her arms to pull her roughly backward.

Lawrence took a step toward Rosie. Instantly she was surrounded by a ring made up of the men, including Barnaby, of the *Ladyship*. If only she believed she could disappear behind them.

''Are you mad?'' Octavia asked. ''You can't mean to release us all, and the *Ladyship,* for . . .''

Without taking his eyes from Rosie, continuing his measured pace in her direction, he replied, ''That's precisely what I mean.''

''I won't allow it,'' Octavia said.

Laughing in astonishment, Lawrence glanced back at her. ''You won't allow it? Really? And how do you intend to prevent it?'' He watched her struggle in the hands of her guards. ''Ah, Octavia,'' he said mockingly, ''are you jealous? Did you think I meant to take you?''

He sauntered back to her and took her chin in his hand. She wrenched it away and he recaptured it, cruelly. ''Perhaps I might have, once.'' Looking at Rosie, he added, ''But now I think I have a better way to hurt your friend Captain Lyons. Such a fine surprise to have it be the *Ladyship* that fell into my trap, and to find her aboard.''

Only then did Rosie notice that the bodies of the seamen were still lying on the deck. Could Lawrence actually have killed some of his own men to use as bait for his trap?

Lawrence's gaze shifted back to Octavia. ''You didn't see the way he looked at her the night of the fire in the Drop Anchor. I fear your days as favorite may be over.'' He lowered his voice. ''Besides, I want her in a way I have never wanted you.'' He squeezed her chin sharply before dropping his hand from her face, then dodged as she spit at him. ''Such an unbecoming emotion, jealousy,'' he murmured to her, turning away. ''You're beautiful, Octavia, but too spare, too cool for my tastes. This one''—he gestured to Rosie—''has fire, even if she doesn't know it. And is far better endowed,'' he added nastily.

The sailors around Rosie tightened their circle. Rosie herself cast a furtive glance over to the *Ladyship,* where Tuti and Tiny stood at the gunwale helplessly watching under the pointed guns of four Royal Marines, their own weapons useless on the deck. She could see no escape. Jumping overboard was futile; she would be fished out, shot or left to drown, none of which was an option that appealed to her. At least while she was alive, there might be some way out.

''Gentlemen,'' Lawrence said, stopping before Rosie and her protectors, ''I advise you to step aside. Otherwise, this will become an exercise in needless violence. If you make any moves that might be misunderstood, my mate will have no choice but to blow off Octavia's beautiful head. I doubt that's a scene you'd like to witness.'' He took another step forward and the sound of the mate's pistol being cocked reverberated in the silence. For a long moment Baptiste continued to stand in front of Rosie, his fists raised in Lawrence's face.

Then Rosie took his arm, comforted by the feel of the hard muscle beneath her fingers, and pushed it down until it hung at his side. She stepped out from behind her defenders and faced Charles Lawrence, recognizing his willingness to sink the *Ladyship* with all hands aboard. She hadn't forgotten her promise to Octavia that sunstruck afternoon on the quarterdeck, that she would do anything she could to help in the search of Raider's brother.

"I'll go with you," Rosie said. "Don't hurt anybody."

Strangely, her voice sounded calm, though she was trembling inside. She lifted her chin high. Octavia was her example and she didn't mean to disgrace herself or shame her friends by cowering. Lawrence's gaze dropped from Rosie's expressionless face to the front of her striped shirt; her fast, frightened breathing caused her breasts to press against the thin fabric. He smiled.

"Very sensible, my dear," he said soothingly. "Very sensible."

"No, Rosie!" Barnaby cried. "Don't go with him. He's bad."

Without turning around, Rosie said, "It's all right, Barnaby."

"No, it isn't! You don't know what he can do."

Rosie, fighting for composure, wished that were true. She'd seen the look of jaunty cruelty on his face and could imagine only too well. "I'll be fine," she said. "Please don't do anything that will get you or anybody else hurt."

Rosie knew she couldn't be responsible for more violence; she had already seen too much. Whatever Lawrence might do to her was worth it if it spared the lives of Tuti, whom she loved, and Octavia, whom she admired; and of Barnaby and Baptiste, Max and Animal and the rest who had taught her and cared for her and helped her, who had been the brothers, the family she had never had.

Oh, but how frightened she was. Her imagination, newly enlarged by Tuti's instruction, fed her images of Charles Lawrence and herself and made her feel nauseated. She banished those images. They weren't helping her to be brave.

Lawrence thrust his gun into his belt and extended his hand to her. When she did not raise hers to meet it, he snatched her hand into his large, hot palm, then enclosed it, pressing his fingers into hers. She could not have felt more imprisoned had she been in chains.

He pulled her across the deck, past the men of the *Lightning* standing alert, their guns trained on Rosie's friends.

"So—our little game of hunt-and-chase can go on," Lawrence said to Octavia, taunting her. Turning to his mate, he ordered, "See that they all return to the *Ladyship*." Bending to Rosie, he murmured, "All except you, pet."

∽∞∽

Chapter 23

The hulls of the two ships creaked and rubbed together as wave action lifted and rolled the vessels. Rosie looked back at her friends as they passed from one ship to the other, and lifted her free hand in a little wave.

When the *Ladyship*'s crew was all back aboard her, they stood along the rail, watching.

"Get your grappling hooks off my ship," Lawrence bellowed.

For a long moment no one moved. And then, slowly, Big Tom began to pull in the hooks. Rosie ached in every part of her spirit as the two ships separated.

Why had she been allowed the luxury of knowing these people who were now so dear to her if she was only to lose them again? But why should they be different? All her life she'd lost the people and the things she loved, beginning with her mother and Aunt Polly, then Father Xavier and Chila, and finally her livelihood, her kitten, her locket. How had she ever had the temerity to hope for a secure life with happy, healthy children? Her destiny was clearly to be something else.

Without her noticing, the *Lightning*'s sails had been spread, and slowly she began to pull away from the

Ladyship in the light night winds. Rosie could not give a name to the despair, the sorrow and the fear that lay on her heart at the sight.

Lawrence strode to the rail, dragging Rosie with him. Across the widening stretch of water he called, "Octavia! I'll be returning soon to Campeche on business for the Crown. Why not send your Captain Lyons after me? I'd be delighted to show him my prize." He laughed, a sound of wicked amusement that rolled across the space between the two ships.

Rosie stood pinned beside Lawrence at the *Lightning*'s port side, watching as they slid away. She could see Tuti, her arm lifted over her head, waving slowly, her other arm around Barnaby's shoulders. The distance between them widened rapidly, until Rosie could no longer make out the figures on the deck of the *Ladyship*.

Charles Lawrence released her hand and touched her on the back of her neck. She shuddered in revulsion, wrenched herself away from his touch and turned to face him.

He was tall, though not as tall as Raider, and broad. His body looked soft under his uniform, in spite of the bright buttons and gold braid that helped to disguise this. He was very fair and his face, instead of tanning from exposure to the sun and sea, had turned pink and somewhat raw.

"And now that you've said your good-byes, my dear, I'd like to show you my cabin." His fingers closed on her upper arm and he took her with him belowdecks.

The corridors of the *Lightning* smelled different from those of the *Ladyship*—not of candle wax and polish and Tuti's herbs, but of gunpowder and sweat and old cooking.

Lawrence turned the brass handle of his cabin door and pushed her inside. It was completely unlike the cabins she had seen aboard the *Ladyship*. There, the

143

living spaces were filled with the personal expressions of the people who lived within them: tools, books, pictures, items of beauty and use and pleasure.

Charles Lawrence's cabin was as bare as if no one lived there. The bunk didn't have a cover, only a rough gray blanket, and the basin and ewer were of plain tin. The two shelves above the desk were empty except for a copy of Bowditch's *Practical Navigator*, and the desk held only charts. Rosie found no clues to his personality in his cabin, unless its very sterility revealed the man who had lived there for so long. The only life apparent was that of the heaving night sea, barely seen through the big window behind the desk.

She stood in the center of the large cabin while he locked the door, pocketed the key and then lounged against the closed door, his hands behind him, inspecting her. "You're very decorative, my dear. Exactly what this poor place has been needing."

"If all you wanted was something decorative," Rosie said, "you could have bought a painting. You didn't need me."

"To be honest, I hadn't intended to take you. My first thought was Octavia. She is thoroughly decorative, but so ... *difficult*. Though taking her would have caused Lyons much distress, and that would have been intensely gratifying. But when I saw you ... you must forgive me, my dear, for though I remembered you from the ill-fated Drop Anchor, I didn't remember you as being so very, *very* decorative. You look the same and yet quite different. Also, somewhat more *pliant* than the lovely Octavia. When I remembered the way gallant Captain Lyons came to your rescue the night of the fire, and the way he looked at you then, I thought perhaps I had found something of even greater value to him than Octavia."

"He didn't look at me any special way," Rosie insisted, thinking at the same time, I'll show *you* who's pliant.

Lawrence shrugged and moved away from the door toward her. "Perhaps not. Perhaps I have deluded myself for my own selfish reasons."

He pulled the *tignon* from her hair and tossed it onto the desk. The glossy spill of her hair tumbled down over her shoulders, reminding her of the day Tuti had cut and washed it for her. She wished Tuti never had. Then her appearance wouldn't have changed enough for Captain Lawrence to notice her.

He wound his finger into one of the soft curls next to her ear and she took a step backward, pulling the curl away from his touch.

"Oh, dear," he said petulantly. "Are you going to make this difficult? I had thought we could be friends." He advanced toward her again and she continued backing up until she encountered the bunk behind her. That was one place she knew she didn't want to be, especially with Charles Lawrence.

As his hands cupped her shoulders, she decided she had only one choice.

She waited until he was so close to her that she could feel the gold buttons on his coat pressing into her, until she could feel the hot breath from his open mouth on her cheek. Then she brought her knee up sharply between his legs.

The effect could have been comical if the situation hadn't been so serious. His eyes and mouth rounded into perfect circles of surprise, then narrowed into crescents of anguish, and he made a sound almost like a cow lowing. His hands jerked off her shoulders to the place where she had kicked him, and he sank to his knees.

The first thought that went through Rosie's mind was a gleeful one: She could hardly wait to tell Animal that she had verified what he had taught her—there *is* one perfect place to kick a man.

Then she remembered that she wasn't likely to be seeing Animal again and that Lawrence wasn't likely to stay disabled forever.

She knew she wasn't strong enough to really hurt him unless she had a weapon, and there was nothing in the bare cabin that she could use. She ran to the door, struggling with the handle, but it was firmly locked. The chances of her being able to get the key from Lawrence's pocket were nonexistent. He was already recovering from her blow and rising to his feet.

The long pistol he had trained on Octavia protruded from his belt, and in the moment before he had regained his feet, Rosie grabbed the handle and yanked it away from him. The weight of the weapon was so surprising, she almost dropped it. It was astonishing to her that he had been able to hold the pistol so nonchalantly aimed at Octavia with only one hand. Using both her hands, she could hardly raise it, and firing it was a mystery totally beyond her. She hoped Lawrence wouldn't know that as she stood before him, straining to hold the wavering weapon still.

He started in her direction, wincing with each step.

"Stop or I'll shoot," she commanded. "I mean it."

He reached out a long arm, grabbed the barrel of the gun and effortlessly wrenched it from her fingers. The twist to her wrists that his movement caused induced hot pain in her barely healed wounds. She gasped in agony and then gasped again as his other hand slapped her cheek so hard her neck snapped back.

"You've made a bad mistake, my dear," Lawrence said grimly. "I'm afraid you're going to have to pay for it."

Rosie held her hand against her injured cheek. She didn't think anything was broken, but her jaw throbbed and she'd bitten her tongue and could taste blood. She knew she should have been frightened to death of him—he was apparently perfectly capable of killing her anytime he wanted to—and until a moment before, she had been. But from somewhere came a powerful anger that drowned her fear. She hated this man. She hated all the things he'd done to her and to the people she cared about and also to the ones she didn't even know: the sailors he'd impressed, the ones whose ships he'd sunk under them. She had never felt such a strong emotion. The force of it erased the pain in her jaw and wrists.

It would be insanity for her to pit herself physically against Lawrence, though every muscle in her body craved that. She would have to harness her hatred and the hot, crazy spurts of fearlessness it engendered in her and wait; wait for a time when she could use it well.

And hope that that time came.

So intent was Rosie on examining her new emotion that she barely felt it when Charles Lawrence, holding both her damaged wrists in one large hand, unlocked the door and pushed her roughly out ahead of him. He took her down another flight of steps into a low-ceilinged, musty corridor, at the end of which was a stout door with a small barred window in it. A young sailor stood stiffly at attention beside the door, a ring of keys resting on the stool in the corner.

"Open the door," Lawrence said. "I have another customer for the brig."

"But she's a girl," the sailor protested, startled into insubordination.

Lawrence drew himself up and leveled his acid glance at the sailor. "Any other time that remark would call for a flogging. Now open the door."

"Aye, aye, sir. I'm sorry, sir," the seaman said, scrambling for the keys. "Thank you, sir."

As the sailor forced the key into the lock, Lawrence leaned down to Rosie, his fingers hard on her upper arms, his face only inches from hers. "A little experiment, my dear. Let's see how long it takes before you beg for my companionship. I'd prefer that to taking you by force. But don't forget, that is my second choice. I don't think I'll have long to wait."

She turned away from him as he leaned closer, but she wasn't fast enough. His full, damp mouth made contact with her lips. The experience was loathsome beyond anything she had ever experienced. He tasted the way she imagined bilge water would. Even as she recoiled from him, some distant recess in her brain registered the knowledge that no, not *every* man's kiss affected her the way that Raider Lyons's had.

Then Lawrence flung Rosie through the open door of the brig with such force that she fell to her hands and knees. The door slammed behind her and she heard the key grate in the lock.

Chapter 24

Rosie could feel her galloping heartbeat throughout her entire body, and the pain in her jaw and wrists returned in strength.

The only light in the room was the diffusion through the barred window of lantern glow from the dim corridor, and that was negligible. Rosie could barely see her own hands on the floor.

Her other senses opened in response, and were savagely assaulted.

The smell was putrid beyond telling: sweat, filth and human waste—and something more. Did pain and terror have an odor? The stench was so strong she could taste it in the back of her throat. She tried to breathe in short, shallow gasps, and still she felt the foulness.

The floorboards beneath her palms were at the same time slimy and gritty. As soon as she was aware of this, she drew back onto her heels and scrubbed her hands down the sides of her skirt.

It was then that she heard the sounds.

At first she thought they were her own fear-driven respirations, but when she held her breath to try to still her panic, the gasping sounds went on.

"Is someone here?" she asked in a whisper.

"Aye," a low male voice said. "There are two of us."

"Who . . . who are you?"

A moan was her answer. She heard the movement of bodies and the sound of metal on metal.

Her eyes gradually adjusting, she searched the darkness and had the sense of shadow within shadow to her right. She edged backward.

The voice came again. "You have no need to fear us. We couldn't do you harm even if we wanted to."

Unreasonably comforted by the assurance in the low voice, she asked, "Why couldn't you?"

"For one, we're in irons. Irons bolted into the wall. For another, we've both been flogged, though Simon worse than me."

Barnaby had described flogging to her one sun-swept afternoon on the foredeck. As she'd listened, sick with horror, she realized he couldn't have witnessed what he was telling her or he would never be able to talk about it with such gusto. The British navy was the worst offender, he'd told her, often whipping men to death for minor infractions.

"Are you . . . ?" She didn't even know what to ask. Her heart contracted in helpless pain for these poor sufferers. The pain she felt in her own wrists and jaw diminished in comparison.

"I'll be all right," the voice said. "I drew only ten lashes this time, for looking at our esteemed Captain Lawrence in a manner he deemed challenging. Simon took sixty." Another moan followed these words.

"Sixty!" she exclaimed. Such cruelty was inconceivable to her. "How long have you been in here?"

"I don't know," the low voice said. "It's difficult to tell night from day in here, and being in agony does queer things to your sense of time. A long time, though. Simon's been here only a few days, I'd guess." A pause. "How are you here?"

"Your Captain Lawrence took me from another ship. He wanted me to—to stay with him in his cabin. I tried to shoot him and he didn't like it."

A short laugh came from the shadows. "I imagine not. And I wish you'd succeeded. He's not *my* Captain Lawrence. He took me from another ship, too."

She realized then that his accent was American, not English. "Were you impressed?" she asked.

"Aye. As was Simon and half the hands aboard. I've tried to escape more times than I can tell you, but I seem to have no talent for it. All it's got me was a turn in Dartmoor. But Mother England's in a bad way now. Too many men dead from all the years of fighting Napoleon, and that war not done yet when the Americans started another. Too few seamen spread too thin, so they let some of us out of prison to aid in the effort. I'm afraid my heart's not in it." His voice sounded infinitely weary.

"I shouldn't think so," she said.

Before she could ask him if he knew anything of an impressed American named Lyons, Simon moaned again.

"Easy, mate," the low voice said.

"Water." A rasping, pain-filled plea.

Rosie heard a splashing sound, the clink of chains, the rustle of clothing. Then a sigh. She could see nothing but shadow in the blackness.

"Is there anything we can do for him?" she asked.

"I doubt there's anything anyone could do for him," the man said. "There's no flesh left on his back and almost no blood left in his veins."

"But can't the guard bring a doctor?"

The prisoner laughed, short and devoid of humor. "Lawrence is not known for his humanity."

Needle pricks tortured Rosie's legs, folded too long into a strained position. Bracing her hands against the door behind her, she slowly stood up, and sensed the

151

ceiling only inches above her head. Turning to the small window, she called "Guard! Guard!"

The young sailor outside the door pressed his face against the bars. "Quiet! Do you want the captain to come back?"

That was the *last* thing she wanted. She lowered her voice. "You have to get some help. There's a very ill man here."

"I don't like listening to him any more than you do," he said, "but there's nothing to be done for him. After a flogging, you either live or you don't. Now keep quiet, or it's more trouble for you."

"I don't believe you," Rosie said. "There must be something you can do."

The guard turned away. "There's nothing."

"Please!" she called after him. "This is terrible!"

"You're wasting your breath," the voice in the darkness said. "Save it. You'll need it. Lawrence doesn't care if Simon dies. Then he can use him to lure some unsuspecting ship into coming close enough to be trapped."

"You mean those dead sailors on the deck died from floggings?"

"Floggings or disease or fighting. It doesn't matter to Lawrence. He has uses for his men, dead or alive. When the dead ones get too ripe, he throws them to the fishes. Sometimes he has to use living sailors, but they're not as good—can't keep still as long."

Rosie's fury still protected her from despair. "How can anyone be like that? It's—" She couldn't think of a word strong enough, even in her colorful Spanish vocabulary, and wished she'd listened more closely to some of the ones Big Tom had used when aggravated beyond endurance.

There was no response from the figure in the gloom. Shaking her head, she asked, "Is there anything to sit on?" The floor was so filthy with unknown accretions, she didn't want to touch it.

"Only the floor," he said. "Come over here by me. Don't worry, I'm harmless."

With her eyes growing accustomed to the gloom, she could see his outline now, leaning against the far wall, and hear the rattle of his chains as he moved. She felt her way across the space between them until she reached him.

"Sit down," he said, patting the floor beside him. "I'm glad for the company. Simon's passed out again." Gingerly she lowered herself to his side, trying to sit in as small a place as possible. "It'd be just as well if he never woke up. The maggots have got into his wounds. He's not going to make it."

"Are you sure?"

The man turned toward her. In the gloom she could see his shaggy head nod. His hair was long and a heavy beard covered his face, but his eyes captured whatever light entered the small cell; and though she couldn't tell what color they were, she could see a gleam of reason and curiosity in them.

Rosie rested her head against the wall. "A month ago I actually stood on a beach, looked out to sea and wished I could leave my home and begin having my own life. And this is what I got."

"I used to do that," the man said. "I was so impatient with the orderly life of schooling and business my family offered me. I did everything I could to liven it up, got into all sorts of trouble. Then I went to sea. Oh, the sights I saw and the good times I had. Lord, I miss those days. But I think now a settled, contented life would look a great deal better to me."

"To me, too. My name's Rosie. What's yours?"

"Rip."

She knew a man named Animal and a man named Wolf, but *Rip*? What did a man have to do to get a

153

name like that? She shuddered to think about it, so she decided not to. She was going to be spending her time with this man for who knew how long and she didn't want to be afraid of him when she'd so far had no indication she should be.

Simon moaned again.

"How are you doing, mate?" Rip asked.

Simon answered only with another moan.

Rosie could see now that Simon lay on his face on the other side of Rip. She could tell he wore no shirt, but other than that, she was grateful for the dimness. She didn't want to know what his back looked like.

Rip tipped up a water can, dampened a cloth that might have been Simon's shirt and swabbed it across Simon's forehead. "He's burning up."

Rosie reached across Rip and laid her hand on Simon's head. "Oh, you're right. There has to be *something* we can do."

She rose and moved next to Simon. Then she sank down to the floor again and took his head into her lap. "At least he shouldn't have to lie in this filth."

"Anna?" the injured man mumbled. "Oh, Anna."

Rosie looked up quickly at Rip.

"Anna's his wife," Rip murmured.

Rosie stroked Simon's feverish forehead. "Yes, Simon, it's Anna."

"Praise God, praise God. I never thought to see you again." His voice was faint and thready. "My dear one." He coughed twice and was silent.

"Simon?" Rosie said.

Rip's fingers moved against Simon's neck. Then he took his wrist. After a moment he released it, and the lifeless hand fell onto Rosie's knee and then slid to the floor.

"Poor bastard," Rip said.

Helpless tears gathered in Rosie's eyes. "He's dead?"

Rip nodded. "Guard!" he yelled.

What little light there was in the brig dimmed as the guard's face filled the window. "What is it this time?" he asked.

"No need for a doctor," Rip told him. "He's dead."

"Oh," the boy responded, sounding as unsure as a child. "I guess I better get somebody to take him out." The face disappeared from the window and Rosie and Rip heard his footsteps retreating down the passage.

They sat in silence for a long time, Simon's head still resting in Rosie's lap.

She thought of how different the words "my dear" had sounded when Simon said them to her, thinking she was Anna, than they had when Captain Lawrence said them to her. Apparently love was potent enough to alter even the meaning of the same words.

Eventually they heard footsteps returning. The key turned in the lock and the guard entered with two sailors.

The light from the open door spread into the cubicle, and Rip, accustomed to semidarkness, closed his eyes against the brightness. The guard stayed in the doorway as the two sailors released Simon from his chains and carried him away.

The moments of light gave Rosie an opportunity to assess her surroundings: the dirt-caked floor, the bucket in the corner and the thin, bearded man beside her. His hair and beard were so filthy she could hardly tell what color they were, nor could she see much of his face. The slope of his wide shoulders indicated a kind of deep fatigue: exhaustion underlaid with strain.

Just before the door closed again, Rip raised his head and murmured, "Good-bye, my friend."

Chapter 25

Rosie woke and, as had happened each time she awakened in the cell, wondered for a confused moment where she was. She had gone from avoiding any more contact with the dirty floor than she could help to sprawling full length on it whenever sleep took her.

She no longer had any sense of day or night, nor did she know whether she slept because she was tired or needful of forgetting or merely bored. One thing she did recognize was that she could have no more suitable companion in such a place, or maybe in any place, than Rip. She wished she could say that she had found Raider's brother in Rip. But even before he told her no one in his family could know what had become of him, she was sure he couldn't be related to Raider, because he was so much nicer than Raider.

"But what if there *was* someone who wanted to rescue you?" she asked. "Someone who was willing to board British ships searching for you? Could he do it?"

"I'd say he was a fool. Or a lunatic. The risk is insane. Even if I had someone who wanted to find me, I would tell them not to try. Never would I want on my conscience the fact that I'd caused another human being the misery of impressment. For that's what would happen. Either that or death. The only way any American gets on a British ship is at gunpoint as a prisoner, or as an attacker with a shipload of cannon behind him—and even that's not a guarantee of success."

How right he was. Rosie had had the benefit of the *Ladyship*'s cannon, and look where she was. And she understood Rip's desire to save anyone he cared about from this fate—she felt the same way about Octavia and her crew. She was glad they weren't here with her, and she wouldn't have wanted them to come after her. It was simply too dangerous.

So apparently it was true; Raider *was* mad, to harbor such an arrogant belief that he could do the impossible.

"I've heard," she said cautiously, in case the guard was listening, "that someone may be trying to find a sailor named Lyons. Do you know anything of such a man?"

There was a long silence. Then Rip sighed and said, "No. Nothing. And whoever it is that's looking for him should stop. It can't be done." Then, after another silence, he said, "I wonder who he knows that's so foolhardy."

Mostly they talked of their childhoods, times that now seemed placid and serene when in fact they had been neither, or of books they had read. Rip told her of going to sea on his father's merchant ships, sailing to Shanghai for silks and ivory and tea—and of his memories of doll-like Chinese ladies.

When she needed silence for her own thoughts, he provided that as well.

His courtesy extended to closing his eyes and stopping his ears whenever she had to use the bucket, and sometimes she thought she was more grateful for that than for any of his other acts of kindness.

Inevitably their conversation turned to the war. Rosie

had by now decided where her sympathies lay—emphatically on the American side, despite her half-English heritage.

"That's not unnatural," Rip told her as they sat side by side in the dark, "considering the treatment you've had from one of the English navy's respected captains."

"Surely they can't all be like him," Rosie said, fingering Animal's tied-knot bracelets around her wrists.

"They aren't. Lord Nelson was a real hero, a man loved and admired by his men. Admired by me as well. I'm a seaman, too, and I'll always admire a man who does that job well. I don't hate Lawrence because he's British. I hate him because he's Lawrence. Choosing sides in this war has to do with justice, not nationality."

"I can't find any way to think impressment is right," Rosie admitted, clasping her arms around her knees. "I can't even imagine how any naval officer could think it would work. Anyone should be able to tell that a man forced to do something he doesn't want to do won't be a good worker."

"So obvious even a babe can see it," Rip said.

"You mean me?" Rosie asked, getting ready to be indignant.

Rip's chains clanked as he put his hand on her arm. "Be easy. I wasn't insulting you. I was recognizing your astuteness. As for being a babe, how old are you?"

"Seventeen. Maybe eighteen by now. My birthday's in the summer and I don't know if it has passed now or not. In Campeche, every girl my age is married. Except for La Señora's ladies, and they don't often get married."

"I'm twenty—or maybe twenty-one by now. Seventeen doesn't seem such an advanced age to me. You probably have time left to learn a few more things. Did you think you were supposed to know everything already?"

She had to laugh. "I'm sorry. I'm sensitive about all I don't know. For most of my life I've had more questions than anybody would answer. I've tried to understand things I couldn't get explanations for, but I was never sure I did. Recently I met some people who didn't mind teaching me things. Interesting things, too. And then Captain Lawrence turned up and spoiled everything. I don't understand why life can't run smoothly and why we can't all have what we want. It usually isn't so very much."

Rip laughed almost like a boy. "I don't think you'll find the answer to that one no matter how long you live or who you ask. Would you like to hear my theory?"

"Of course." She loved to hear anyone's theory on anything. She pushed greasy strands of her hair off her forehead and prepared to listen.

"All right. Here it is. How do you know you're having a good run if you haven't had a bad one to contrast it with?"

She waited for more, but nothing more appeared to be forthcoming. "That's your theory?" she finally asked. "Bad times are only so we'll appreciate good times? Why do we have to know they're good times? Why can't we just think this is what life is?"

Rip laughed again. "I can see why people don't want to answer your questions. You don't ask easy ones. It's too bad you can't talk to my big brother. He's dead now, but he read everything and could lecture on any subject until you fell asleep. My sister, I think, was even smarter, but she died, too, when she was just seventeen. Me, I think you do your best and roll with what comes. Someone else is in charge of the whole great show and I hope it makes sense to Him, because it surely does not to me."

"Me, either," Rosie said. "But I suppose you are right about the bad times and the bad people making

159

you appreciate the good ones." She leaned her head against the wall. "Don't you sometimes think you'll lose your mind in here? With the darkness and the closeness and the filth, and not knowing when you'll get out and what will happen to you when you do?"

"I'd be a fool if I didn't think of that. And sometimes I wish I were a fool."

"What do you do to keep your sanity?" Rosie felt her hatred for Charles Lawrence was insulation enough against madness, at least for now. But she wanted information for later, if she should need it.

"I go inside," Rip said. "I remember and I hope. I haven't given up. I don't know what it is that keeps me from it, but it hasn't happened yet. Being alone in here was the worst time. I hate the fact that you have to be here, but for my sake, I'm glad you are."

"I feel the same way." She paused, a little surprised at the affection she felt for a man she probably wouldn't have recognized shaved and in a lighted room. "Tell me something you remember that helps you stay sane."

"Ah, what I remember," he said, sounding pleased. "I start with my first memories, the first things I noticed as a child: the delicious way my mother smelled, like orange blossoms; the sound of the mockingbird outside my window. Its song is called *voix d'amour*—voice of love—and can be so sweet. The foods of my childhood—pralines and ginger cake, sherbet we bought from vendors when my parents took us to walk on the levee at sunset, crawfish bisque and oyster gumbo. And music. Nobody loves music the way they do in New Orleans. My nursemaid sang to me and told me stories I can remember still."

"Would you tell me one?"

"I'll tell you my favorite. When I was small, I was afraid of spiders—especially the Golden Ladies. They were so big and strong; they could throw their webs between trees so far apart, you'd say it was impossible. And they did it over again every night. They came out at dusk and I could imagine them spending the whole night wrapping my house in a giant web so thick and tight I'd never get out. I'd be trapped in there and become a meal for the Golden Ladies. So my nurse told me the story of a wealthy planter whose house was at the end of a two-mile-long allee of oaks. He had two beautiful daughters who fell in love with men he approved of and he wanted to give them the most lavish double wedding he could concoct. He gathered all the Golden Ladies he could find and released them into the trees. After they had spun their huge, elaborate webs, he sprinkled them with gold and silver dust from a special bellows, and when the wedding parties came along the road after dark, by candlelight, the webs shone and sparkled like magic. And in every web sat a proud, maternal Golden Lady, loving the wedding festivities as much as any mother of the bride. After that, spiders didn't seem at all malicious to me. They reminded me of my mother—busy, talented, proud, a little vain, but beautiful enough and smart enough to justify it.''

Rosie could imagine the magic spiderwebs. What a wonderful gift for a father to give his daughters. How she wished she'd had a father who would have thought of such a thing, even if he couldn't arrange it. And how she wished she'd have a daughter someday to do something that wonderful for.

As they sat in silence, thinking of the beautiful spiderwebs, the light from the door's barred window dimmed, an indication that someone stood there.

It was Lawrence.

"Well, my dear, are you ready yet?'' he asked.

"I'll never be ready,'' Rosie answered, hardly raising her voice. She'd given him this answer so many times already, she didn't know why he still asked. Each time he appeared at the door, she was sure this would be the time he would drag her away by force; she hadn't forgotten that was his second choice. But there was not any possibility that she could ever bring herself to go with him voluntarily.

"This is the last time I'll ask," Lawrence said into the dark cell. "Next time you come with me. I've told you what my second choice is. Think about it." And he was gone.

"Oh, if there was only some way I could get off this ship before the next time," Rosie said to Rip. She had no doubt whatsoever that Charles Lawrence would do to her what he had threatened.

A short laugh answered her. "Good luck. I've tried them all."

Rosie shook her head and felt the greasy strings of her hair move against her neck. "I know. I can't swim. I can't row a boat. I can't—"

"You can't get out of here to even try to escape, so why torment yourself? Still, the thought of him with you . . ." He left unfinished whatever his thoughts on the matter were.

Rosie didn't see how they could be any worse than her own.

Chapter 26

As she lay, her cheek on the rough floorboards, Rosie realized what had awakened her. Instead of the pitching of a ship at sea, she felt only the gentle bobbing of a ship lying at anchor.

Sitting up sharply, she asked, "Rip, are you awake?"

She heard the clink of chains. "Yes. We've anchored."

"We must be in Campeche." She stood and shook out her rumpled skirt. "I heard Lawrence say he was going there for a meeting. If only I could tell where we're anchored. I know every inch of this harbor. I *know* there's a way for me to get home." She wouldn't think right now of what home meant. All she knew was that she had to get away from Charles Lawrence. And take Rip with her, if she could.

"I used to think that, too," Rip said.

"But you haven't given up. No, you haven't," she insisted when he was silent. "And I won't, either."

The sound of voices in the corridor stopped their conversation, and then a key turned in the lock. The door swung open and the bulky form of Charles Lawrence filled the opening.

"I told you, my dear, that this time there'd be no discussion," he said. "Come here."

"No," Rosie said.

"I didn't ask. I'm telling you. Come here."

She sat down, wrapped her arms around her knees and lowered her head, trying in some senseless way to attach herself to the floor.

"Why don't you leave her alone, Lawrence?" Rip asked. "What pleasure is there in taking a girl who's revolted by you?"

Lawrence strode inside to stand before Rip, took a long, measuring look at him and then struck him in the face with the back of his hand. Rip's head hit the wall and fell forward. In the light from the open door, Rosie could see a thin line of blood running out of the corner of Rip's mouth and the glisten of barely leashed violence in his eyes.

"I wonder how you'd like a few more stripes on your back," Lawrence said. Then he laughed. "I think depriving you of your little companion will be torture enough. For now." He bent, took Rosie by the arm and yanked her to her feet. "I have plans for you, my dear."

The very touch of his hand on her arm caused her skin to crawl, but the harder she tried to pull away from him, the more tightly his fingers dug into her flesh. Before she could say even a word of farewell to Rip, she was dragged into the corridor and toward the steps to the next deck. As she heard the cell door close behind her, she marveled that already she was thinking of that pestilential place as a haven.

Lawrence didn't release his hold on her until he had pushed her into his cabin and locked the door behind him.

"God, you stink," he said to her.

"What did you expect?" she retorted. "I haven't

seen a drop of water in who knows how long, except for that scrummy stuff we were expected to drink."

She was conscious for the first time of her own rank odor and, looking down, saw crusted filth on her arms and hands and under her nails. A flicker of hope rose in her. Maybe now he would no longer want her. Maybe now he would go ashore and get one of La Señora's ladies to entertain him, though she felt sorry for whichever one had to do it.

Perhaps sensing her hopefulness, he said, "There's nothing wrong with you that a bath and some decent clothes won't fix."

He gestured and she saw, in the corner of the cabin, an oval tin tub filled with steaming water.

"I don't want a bath," she said.

He laughed. "Not much, you don't. I have to go ashore, but I'll be back. When I return, I want to find you waiting for me, clean and dressed in those." He pointed to the bunk, on which Rosie saw a pile of women's clothing neatly folded.

"Never," she said. "I'll be just as dirty and smelly when you come back as I am now." If I'm even here when you get back, she thought to herself.

Lawrence moved to the desk and lit the lamp there. "Then I'll be forced to wash you myself, a task I rather look forward to. Think of it, my dear, of how I will reveal every pink inch of you."

Grabbing her face roughly with both hands, he kissed her, wetly and invasively.

Rosie jerked away and wiped the back of her hand across her lips. "That was disgusting," she said through gritted teeth.

"I'll have to educate you, I can see. How much better you'll taste clean," he said and, laughing, turned and left the cabin, locking the door behind him. She was there in an instant, rattling the latch, trying to force the door open. She could hear Lawrence's laugh receding down the corridor.

The last rays of the setting sun streamed through the spray-filmed window behind the desk, striping the bare floor with bands of gold.

After so long in darkness, Rosie thought the touch of one of those golden bars across her chest was almost intoxicating.

To be alone in a clean, well-lit room, no matter whose it was, was a luxury she had almost forgotten. She crossed to the window and looked out across the water to the harbor of Campeche. Between the failing light and the dirty window, she could distinguish frustratingly little, but she could tell where she was. The placement of the *Lightning* prevented her from seeing the site of the Drop Anchor, but she could picture it and remember it as it had been in what seemed like a life belonging to someone else.

She watched the harbor dim into darkness and saw lights come on in the ships riding at anchor. A few lights flickered on shore along the great wall that surrounded the town. Sighing, she turned away from the window. Even if she broke it open, even if she jumped from it, she still couldn't swim. There was no way to get to shore.

She clenched her filthy hands and tears of defeat gathered in her eyes.

The steaming tub invited her to come closer. She rubbed her dirty hands together and thought no harm could come from washing them. As long as the rest of her remained rank, she could still hope to think of some way to fend off Lawrence's attentions.

She knelt beside the tub, removed Animal's bracelets and plunged her hands into the water.

Bliss.

There was a cake of scented soap and a cloth in a

bowl beside the tub. Rosie took the soap and lathered it into piles of bubbles, covering her hands and the raw red scars on her wrists. The bubbles smelled of spice and lemon. Unable to help herself, she smoothed the lather up over her arms. When the sleeves of her shirt became wet, she pulled the shirt off and continued spreading the foam over her shoulders and chest.

Before she knew it, she had stripped off the rest of her dirty clothing and, leaving it in a pile on the floor, had climbed into the tub. The warm water, scented soap and privacy were more than she could resist. She reasoned that she could always put her old clothes back on before Lawrence returned, and be as repugnant as she had been before. Besides, she deserved this. If she couldn't actually escape, at least she could indulge herself in this tiny, temporary liberation.

She washed her hair and soaked until the water cooled. Dried and wrapped in the towel, she went over to the bunk to inspect the clothes that Lawrence had left for her.

Around her, she could hear the sounds of shipboard life familiar to her from her time on the *Ladyship:* the creak of ropes, sailors' footsteps and voices, metal on metal. Now that she was warm and clean, the sounds induced in her a false sense of well-being.

Lifting a sheer lawn chemise edged with delicate embroidery and fitted with a satin ribbon drawstring, she inhaled with pleasure. The workmanship was exquisite. She slipped it over her head and tied the ribbon in the front. It was like wearing a whisper, a cloud.

Heady with pleasure, she stepped into a snowy petticoat deeply edged with lace, then pulled on the high-waisted gown of cornflower-blue silk, trimmed with velvet ribbons the color of lapis and fastened up the back with a long line of tiny brass hooks. There were even slippers of lapis-colored satin.

She would wear them only for a moment, she told herself, only to see how she looked, to feel how such garments felt. Shaking her damp hair back over her shoulders, she stood in front of the dark window, where her reflection in the yellow lamplight looked back at her.

She hardly knew herself.

Her eyes were wide and dark, her cheeks pinked from the heat of the bath, her shoulders pearly against the silk of the dress. And her bosom, something she'd never paid much attention to before, looked, well . . . womanly.

She crossed her hands over her chest and the color in her cheeks deepened. Charles Lawrence was the last person in the world she wanted to see her looking like this.

It pained her to think of removing the elegant clothes and replacing them with her own ragged ones, but she knew there was no choice.

As she turned away from the window, she heard a low footfall outside the door. The handle turned slowly and then was released.

Chapter 27

Panicked, knowing only that she had to get out of the dress before Lawrence returned, she struggled to unfasten the tiny hooks down the back. Haste made her clumsy and she'd undone only three or four when a rasping sound came from the door's lock and the door opened inward.

Rosie stood in the center of the room, her arms twisted up behind her back, still wrestling with the fastenings, when Raider Lyons and Nicodemus McNair stepped inside.

As Nicodemus closed the door behind them, Raider took a long look at her and said, "Good God. You little fool."

"What?" She was so stunned she thought he must be a hallucination. Yet he looked entirely real—the tight, tanned skin; the vivid eyes; the long, fluent body.

He held a pistol, and so did Nicodemus McNair.

Nicodemus McNair? Her imagination must be better than she'd even dreamed.

"It didn't take him long to turn you into his trollop," Raider said in a voice he fought to keep level.

Hot anger flooded Rosie as she realized this was no

trick of her imagination. She could never conceive of him saying such a thing to her.

"How dare you!" she cried, outraged.

In one swift movement he was beside her, his right arm around her waist and his left palm over her mouth. She'd been manhandled enough for one day, and the indignity of his assumption coupled with the discomfort of his hold on her broke the last of her control. She clawed at his wrist, kicked the little satin slippers against his shins and fought him like a cornered animal.

"Quiet," he ordered, tightening his grip painfully. "Do you want the whole of Lawrence's crew to descend on us? Whatever other plans you may have had for the evening, I'm here to rescue you, whether you want it or not. We've not gone to all the trouble of getting aboard undetected to leave empty-handed."

She never thought she'd be so affronted by a rescuer, but his attitude was insufferable and he was hurting her. Still, he had mentioned leaving the *Lightning,* which was something she was definitely in favor of. Later she could give him the piece of her mind that she'd already set aside for him.

Nicodemus had been going through Lawrence's desk drawers. He pulled out a ledger book, flipped hastily through it, scanning the pages, then shut it in disgust. "Nothing but columns of the words 'Common Seaman', with no names. There's no way to know if he's aboard." His scarred face was eerie in the wavering lamplight. "We've got to hurry."

Raider leaned forward to speak against Rosie's ear. "Are you coming easily or not?" Then he pressed his cheek against her damp curls and said, "Or do you want to stay?"

Wrenching her face from the captivity of his hand, Rosie whispered furiously, unable to save that piece of her mind any longer, "Of course I don't want to stay! How could you even think such a—"

"Then come on," he interrupted, his arm still around her waist, pulling her to the door, which Nicodemus had silently opened. "Keep quiet and do exactly as I tell you." He pushed her ahead of him through the door.

The passage was dim and quiet and no one was in sight. At the end of the corridor was the flight of steps that led to the upper deck.

How they had managed to get aboard without being seen was beyond Rosie, unless most of the crew were ashore with their captain. Or drunk. Or asleep. Or just didn't care, if they all felt the way Rip did about serving under Charles Lawrence.

Rip! She couldn't escape without Rip.

"Wait," she whispered. "There's someone—" From behind her, Nicodemus's huge hand pulled her back against him and covered her mouth and most of her nose, so that she could hardly breathe. He held her so as she struggled more and more weakly and saw black spots swim before her eyes while, silently, Raider stole ahead to take a cautious look around. Then he beckoned to Nic to follow him.

Before Nic removed his hand from Rosie's mouth, he whispered in her ear, "Another sound and I'll break your neck. Dinna think I cannot. The only words I want from you are if you've encountered a sailor named Lyons. If you have not, you are to keep quiet."

He released her and Rosie wavered, breathing deeply as her personal solar system faded. She did indeed believe that Nicodemus McNair could break her neck. But Rip—she couldn't go without trying again to save him, too, even if he wasn't Raider's brother.

"You don't understand," Rosie began.

The look on McNair's face could have turned back a tide. And he was raising his hands to her neck.

She hurried on. "There's a sailor in the brig—"

"And that's where he'll be staying," he whispered, pushing her along the corridor, "unless he's who we're looking for."

"He's not, but he's—"

Nicodemus's big hand went around her neck, cutting off speech and almost breath. "Shut. Up. Can you understand that much? Why Raider wanted to come after you . . ." He shook his head, loosened his grip slightly and pushed her ahead of him, having finally frightened her into silence.

Raising his voice slightly, he said to Raider, "Where now?"

"The gun deck. The forecastle. Those are the most likely places."

Soundless as shadows, they moved through the passage and down to the gun deck, which was silent and empty, the cannons standing ominous and evil at their ports.

"All ashore?" Nicodemus asked.

"Possibly," Raider replied. "There's not as much danger of desertion here as in ports not surrounded by jungle. Let's try the forecastle."

Rosie allowed herself to be towed along, Nicodemus holding her wrist in an iron grasp. Looking for Raider's brother, who probably wasn't even still alive, seemed such an exercise in futility when there was Rip, perfectly deserving, so close by and so in need of rescue, and she could get neither Raider nor Nicodemus to listen to her plea for him.

The dim light of one lantern was the only illumination in the forecastle: after dark, most sailors who weren't sleeping preferred to be on deck. While Nic and Rosie waited, Raider silently eased himself between the hammocks, peering into the sleeping faces, freezing when a man groaned and turned in his sleep.

Raider took his time, a long, slow time, while prickles of fear ran along Rosie's spine as she expected Charles Lawrence at any moment to come up behind her. But she didn't say anything. She hardly thought Nicodemus McNair would be sympathetic.

Finally Raider returned to them, shaking his head. "He's not there," he said. "He could be ashore. Or anywhere." His shoulders were held in a defeated line and his mouth was flat and grim.

"We should go now," Nicodemus said.

Raider didn't move, his thoughts elsewhere, his eyes remote.

"Raider," Nic said. "We canna stay. We've been too long already."

A moment passed before Raider's eyes came alive again, and then he spoke. "You're right. I'd only hoped . . ." His voice trailed off.

"Aye. I know. There'll be another time."

"Of course," Raider said tautly, doubt coloring his words. He turned and led them carefully back to the companionway leading to the deck.

Once on deck, they hunched behind a cluster of barrels and listened. The night air was warm and heavy and Rosie breathed fast through her open mouth. Somehow the air didn't seem to be reaching her lungs.

Raider's whisper came into her ear. "Our boat's tied at the stern. We'll have to traverse the whole of the ship to get to it. Follow me."

He moved, a barely discernible shadow in the darkness. She darted after him, feeling clumsy and too visible, and Nicodemus followed her, huge and silent.

Across the deck of the *Lightning*, two sailors, apparently on watch, leaned against the rail, smoking and looking toward the harbor.

Nic, Rosie and Raider inched stealthily toward the stern, stopping each time they came to a barrier big

173

enough to hide them until they felt it was safe to move again. The normal ship sounds of creaking timbers and water slapping on wood were enough to cover whatever small sounds they made as they moved.

Their escape seemed to Rosie to be taking forever. She didn't see why they couldn't have taken a few more minutes to go get Rip. The logistics of getting past whoever was guarding the brig seemed negligible to her, as long as Nicodemus was along.

As they crouched behind a pile of sails waiting to be mended, they heard the sound of oars on water and then the thump of a boat hitting the side of the frigate. Voices echoed in the tropical darkness and there was the tread of boots on the deck.

A chill ran along Rosie's hot skin when she heard Lawrence's voice asking, "Who in blazes has left a skiff tied at the stern? Do I have to do the thinking for everybody on this blasted ship? I've got something better waiting for me than the job of tracking down some idiot pretending to be a sailor."

Chapter 28

Running footsteps sounded, headed for the stern. Raider's whisper came, barely loud enough to be heard. "We'll have to make a break for it. Otherwise there'll be no boat to leave in. Stay close." His shadow rose and swiftly moved away from them.

Nic's fingers grasped Rosie's upper arm and he pulled her with him as he followed Raider. Her feet, awkward in the unfamiliar new shoes, tangled in the fabric of her skirt and she fell almost to her knees before Nic's strong hand jerked her upright.

But her involuntary cry of dismay had not gone unheard.

"Who's there?" Lawrence called. She heard his boots moving on the deck and his voice coming closer as the three of them ran to the stern. "Stop! Guards! Get more light up here!"

A lantern appeared on the deck, then another, and then the thunder of feet as it seemed everybody on board was running in the same direction. Raider reached the taffrail barely ahead of two sailors, but before he could sling his leg over the side, they caught him. A second later Lawrence arrived, his saber drawn. He stood before Raider as a half circle of sailors gathered to press the three fugitives back against the rail.

Lawrence's mouth stretched into a grim smile. "Lyons. I've been wondering when you'd turn up. I felt sure you'd follow the bait."

Nicodemus had released his hold on Rosie's arm; and oddly, she missed the warmth of his hand.

Seeing one of his sailors train a pistol on Raider, Lawrence barked, "No guns, you fool. This is a neutral port. We must handle this problem quietly. With blades."

Touching the tip of his saber lightly to the part of Raider's chest exposed by his unbuttoned shirt, Lawrence turned to Rosie. "I can't tell you how disappointed I am, my dear, that you've chosen to make off with *this*"—he pressed the point against Raider's flesh until a drop of blood appeared—"instead of remaining with me. You look quite charming, by the way. I knew that color would suit you." He was silent for a moment and then, as if musing, he continued. "Perhaps there's a way I could persuade you to stay." He pressed the saber's point harder and a trickle of blood wove through the hairs on Raider's chest and slid down inside his shirt. "I once regretted not sinking the *Polaris*," he said to Raider. "But if I had, think how much sport with you I would have missed."

"Stop it!" Rosie cried. She looked at Raider, but his face showed nothing, as impassive as if he were merely an observer. "What kind of a—a *thing* are you?" She wished again for some of Big Tom's worst words.

"Does this mean," Lawrence asked, "that you wouldn't be willing to trade your favors for the life of Captain Lyons?" He poked again with the point of his weapon and a fresh gout of blood appeared on Raider's chest. Still Raider's face remained unmoved, the bones as immobile as if stone.

Then Nicodemus spoke. "Would you make a bargain with the devil, lass? This man's word means nothing. He's just as like to kill us all, no matter what he says he'll do." Nicodemus himself could have been the devil, with his dreadful scar and the white streaks in his hair and beard.

Rosie caught a glance between Nic and Raider, the merest flick of expressive eyes, but she had the sense that some information had been exchanged, some plan approved.

Once again Nic took hold of Rosie's arm, and the grasp of his fingers was like steel. A fleeting thought flowed through her mind that if she survived this night, tomorrow would see her so spotted with bruises as to resemble an ocelot from the jungles beyond Campeche.

Lawrence continued to look at Rosie with an air of expectancy, his crew ranged around him.

From the corner of her eye she sensed Raider take a small step backward, something she would have done long before had a sword point been pressing into her chest. At almost the same moment Lawrence lunged forward, his saber extended.

Just as she saw the point of the blade touch Raider's side, Nicodemus was pushing her over the taffrail, his large body following her, his arm clamped around her waist. Desperately she clawed for something to cling to, to stop her fall. Her fingers brushed a rope and she grabbed it. At the same time Nicodemus McNair's hand clamped onto it, too. Their plummet slowed with a jerk and, with his arm still around her, they slid toward the water, the rope burning through Rosie's palms.

Nic's boots struck the side of the skiff with a thud and then, just as her own feet touched the little boat, the rope loosened in her hands and she fell with relief into a puddle of water in the bottom of the boat. If it

177

had been the sea, she would have endured this unexpected rescue only to drown before it was completed.

Raider fell on top of her, knocking her painfully against edges and corners she couldn't see. There was shouting from above, and objects she couldn't identify fell, splashing in the water, one hitting her in the temple.

The cut end of the rope was still clutched in Raider's hands as Nicodemus pushed away from the side of the *Lightning*.

Lacking his usual grace, Raider disentangled himself from Rosie, pulled himself to a seat and grabbed an oar. As he and Nic put their backs into their rowing, the skiff drew away from the frigate with surprising swiftness. A single shot struck the water beside the boat and Rosie heard, at a distance, Lawrence's voice shouting, "No guns, I told you, you infernal ass!"

It was wet in the bottom of the boat where she sat, Raider's booted feet on either side of her hips, his knees beside her ears and though the night breeze was warm, Rosie shivered and hugged herself with her rope-burned hands, her wrists aching.

"Do you think they'll follow us?" she asked.

"Nay" Nic answered. "He'd rather meet us in full daylight on the open sea, guns blazing. And he'll doubtless get the chance, since he'll be looking for us harder than ever now. We'd be best to up anchor immediately, eh, Raider?"

His voice low and strained, Raider answered, "An excellent idea. Even if we have to kedge to get away with so little wind, we're better off not to wait until morning."

Nic turned his head to look back at Raider. "Those little nicks of Lawrence's bothering you?"

"It's not the little nicks," Raider answered. "It's the big one."

"What big one?" Nic asked.

The dark bulk of a ship loomed in front of them, and as they drifted past the bow, Rosie saw the word "Avenger" painted on the hull. Raider's crew must have been awaiting them, for a boarding ladder immediately dropped overboard, its end floating on the black water.

Nic grabbed the ladder and said to Rosie, "Get up there. Fast."

It didn't seem to matter that Lawrence would be after them, blazing guns and all. Climbing aboard the *Avenger,* a place she had never been before, Rosie had a sense of homecoming, with the terrifying Nicodemus McNair and the maddening Robert Lyons as her angels of salvation.

Though she had many reasons to distrust and fear Raider and Nicodemus, she knew that not only had they saved her virtue and perhaps her life, but, through them, she would almost certainly once again see Tuti and Octavia, Barnaby and Baptiste, and the rest of the *Ladyship*'s crew. They were all a part of the new life she was embarked upon. And though she didn't know where her life would now take her, as no one does, it had been enhanced and expanded by these people she had met under such difficult circumstances, but who had been so generous to her. If she had to tolerate Raider's rudeness and Nic's threats to get back to those on the *Ladyship,* it was no hardship.

Every pleasure had its price, and as Rip had told her, the bad times made the good ones all the sweeter.

Afterword

The word "Cajun" is a frontier corruption of the word "Acadian," as "Injun" is a corruption of Indian. The Acadians originally came from Nova Scotia to Louisiana in 1755; the word "Cajun" did not come into recorded usage until 1868. I am using it in this book set in 1814 because it is now a more familiar word to us than Acadian, and because it was probably in colloquial use before it was in recorded use, though no one can say how long ago that was.

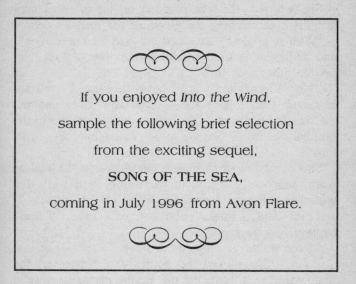

If you enjoyed *Into the Wind*,

sample the following brief selection

from the exciting sequel,

SONG OF THE SEA,

coming in July 1996 from Avon Flare.

Sunrise and sunset were Rosie's favorite times. They were periods of change, and her interest in them seemed appropriate. From the long, west-facing windows in Raider's room she could only sense the coming of dawn, the gradual lifting of darkness by mists of gray and pink and gold. But she could see the sunsets—displays of extravagant tropical colors so flamboyant she was tempted to step through the French doors onto the gallery and scold the twilight for its lack of restraint.

On the fifth day, she'd abandoned the nankeen dress to the workbasket beside her chair and gone to the windows to watch the changing sky of dusk. As she stood, limned in vivid colors, she heard the rustle of bedclothes and then a low voice, hoarse from disuse.

"*Now* am I dead?" he asked.

She whirled. He was propped on his elbow facing her, his eyes catching the gleam of the sunset's colors.

"You're awake!" she cried, so glad for his recovery, and at the same time wistful at the loss of her quiet private times with him. "I'll go get Tuti."

"No. Why should you? I have the sense I need her less now than I have for several days. Stay and tell me what's happened." He looked around, taking in the familiar setting. "So we're at The Cove. For how long?"

She came toward him and stood beside the bed as warm shadows gathered in the room, even while the windows still held dwindling shades of dusk-down.

"Five days, I think." She laughed a little. "I seem to have lost track, too."

"I remember you told me a story."

"Yes." She moved the bottles and glasses on the night table. "It came to me in the strangest way. I didn't even know I knew it."

"Tuti always says the best surprises come from yourself." His voice had gathered strength but retained a distant, musing quality.

She knew she should test his forehead for fever but touching him awake was not at all the same thing as touching him asleep, and she couldn't do it. "Is your fever gone?" she asked.

"Apparently," he said, wincing as he shifted position. He lowered the sheet to inspect his wound and, seeing the size of the bandage, said, "I expect I'm going to have an interesting scar." In the last of the light Rosie could just detect his smile. "I'm sure Barnaby can hardly wait to see it."

She smiled in return. How well he knew the little powder boy. She couldn't make herself believe this was a young man with no heart. But he had, for some reason, barriers around his heart—which for all practical purposes was the same thing as having no heart, she reminded herself.

She turned from the bed. "I must light the candles. And get Tuti. She'll be so relieved you're awake."

"Don't light the candles. And don't get Tuti. Or anybody. Not yet. Come sit with me."

He'd been ill, she told herself. Perhaps close to death. Wasn't he thus entitled to a moment of indulgence before returning to relentless duty? Still not facing him, she asked, "But aren't you hungry? Don't you want to see"—she hesitated—"Octavia?"

"In good time. Come Surely you won't deny a recovering man his first wish." After a pause he added, "I remember the touch of your cool hands on my head during the fever."

"That could have been Tuti. Or Octavia," Rosie said, forcing herself to remember Frank's warnings about Raider's charm and power.

"They were yours. Don't be afraid for me. I feel quite robust. A week's sleep is just what I was needing." When she didn't reply, he said, "Are you still angry about the way I greeted you in Lawrence's cabin?"

That caused her to turn to him. "I'm glad you reminded me of that," she said, indignation returning to her voice. "It was very rude of you, especially when you didn't know the reason I was there."

"Why *were* you there?" He sounded only mildly curious, but Rosie sensed a more urgent interest beneath his words. She'd learned in the brig with Rip that darkness opened her senses to nuances she missed when her eyes could see—and be distracted.

Fiercely, she said, "Because he'd gotten tired of waiting for me to beg him to let me out of the brig and he came and dragged me to his cabin. He left a hot bath and clean clothes to tempt me when he went ashore and . . .'' Her ferocity failed when she remembered how easily she'd succumbed to those temptations.

"You couldn't resist," he finished for her. "Very understandable." She detected sympathy in his low voice. "I've been filthy enough in my time to appreciate the impulse. You're right; it was rude of me. I apologize."

As he said the words he remembered the murderous spurt of rage he'd felt when he opened the door to Lawrence's cabin and found her there, sweet and perfumed in courtesan's clothing. Through his black wrath, he'd reminded himself that she was only a tavern wench who'd undoubtedly been with men far less appealing than Lawrence. But woven through that thought, like a silver fish through a stormy sea, was the memory of her guileless, flustered kiss the night of the tavern fire, and his certainty that it was her first. The relief he felt at her explanation for her presence in Lawrence's cabin was as baffling as his anger on finding her there to begin with.